Paper Hearts

Meg Wiviott

PAPER HEARTS

Margaret K. McElderry Books
New York London Toronto Sydney New Delhi

MARGARET K. McELDERRY BOOKS
An imprint of Simon & Schuster Children's Publishing Division
1230 Avenue of the Americas, New York, New York 10020
This book is a work of fiction. Any references to historical events, real people, or
real places are used fictitiously. Other names, characters, places, and events are
products of the author's imagination, and any resemblance to actual events or
places or persons, living or dead, is entirely coincidental.
Text copyright © 2015 by Meg Wiviott
Jacket photo-illustration and design by Sonia Chaghatzbanian
All rights reserved, including the right of reproduction in whole or in part in
any form.
MARGARET K. McELDERRY BOOKS is a trademark of Simon & Schuster, Inc.
For information about special discounts for bulk purchases, please
contact Simon & Schuster Special Sales at 1-866-506-1949 or business
@simonandschuster.com.
The Simon & Schuster Speakers Bureau can bring authors to your live
event. For more information or to book an event, contact the Simon &
Schuster Speakers Bureau at 1-866-248-3049 or visit our website at
www.simonspeakers.com.
Book design by Sonia Chaghatzbanian and Irene Metaxatos
The text for this book is set in Adobe Garamond Pro.
Manufactured in the United States of America
10 9 8 7 6 5 4 3 2 1
CIP data is available from the Library of Congress.
ISBN 978-1-4814-3983-1 (hardcover)
ISBN 978-1-4814-3985-5 (eBook)

FIRST
EDITION

for Fania & Zlatka

Berta
Bronia
Cesia
Eva Pany
Fela
Giza
Guta
Hanka
Hanka W
Hélène
Irena
Mala
Mania
Mazal
Mina
Rachela
Ruth
Tonia

Acknowledgments

My heart is filled with the people to whom I owe thanks: Judye Groner, who first brought the Heart from Auschwitz to my attention; Luc Cyr at Ad Hoc Films; Julie Guinard, Museum and Collection Coordinator at the Montreal Holocaust Memorial Centre, for all her support and assistance, and for granting permissions to use photos and the messages from the Heart; and Sandy Fainer, who is as patient and kind as her mother, Fania.

None of this would have been possible without the the Vermont College of Fine Arts community, particularly Rita Williams Garcia and Shelley Tanaka, who read drafts of this story when it was fresh from the primordial ooze. Thanks are also due to Caroline Carlson, Gale Jacob, Hannah Moderow, Lori Steel, Kathleen Wilson, and Morgan Zubof, who read versions at various stages. Also, thank you to my workshop group at the 2013 VCFA Novel Writing for Young People Retreat: Rob Costello, Catey Miller, and Amy

Kolb Noyes. Heartfelt thanks to Melanie Crowder, who provided daily check-ins during drafting.

I owe special gratitude to Rabbi Don Rossoff, who generously took time to explain variations in Yiddish and Hebrew transliterations as well as the nuances in the *Unetaneh Tokef* and the *Shema*, and also reviewed the glossary. Any errors are mine and are not a reflection of his teaching.

Thank you to Janine Le, agent extraordinaire, who believed in this story—and me.

Thanks to everyone at Margaret K. McElderry Books: Karen Wojtyla for loving this story, Annie Nybo for answering frantic emails, Erica Stahler for brilliant and thorough copyediting, and Sonia Chaghatzbanian for giving Fania and Zlatka the perfect cover.

Thank you to Morgan and Noah, who have always believed in me.

Finally—and always—to Jim, who holds my heart.

Paper Hearts

Zlatka

Prużany Ghetto

Through the village
   once loved.
Eyes lowered
   not shamed
footsteps steady
   not faster
        or slower
   than before.

Ignored jeers.
Ignored curses,
   Brudny Żyd!
   Dirty Jew!
The clump of mud
thrown by Oleg Broz
   who'd gone to the same school as me
   whose father worked at the same bank as me.

I never
   covered the accursed yellow armband.
But I never
   looked my tormentors in the eye.
I knew better
   than to glare at an angry bull.

My throat grew thick
   with swallowed tears
as I passed
the school
   forbidden,
the synagogue
   empty,
friends' homes
   vacant.

Clenched fists
hid in my pockets
as I passed
the German guards.

My village
had become
a nightmare
   a ghetto.
A monster that held Jews
in its barbed-wire belly.
Let out only

to work
for slave wages,
or in death
    exhaustion
    disease
    starvation.

I hurried home
looking past the barbed wire
to the horizon
  the sunset
still beautiful.

The Germans Arrived

in June of 1941
  the beginning of summer
when hope
  should have
hung in blue-filled skies.
But hope burned away
in the heat of summer.

First came the yellow armbands
  branding all us Jews.

Then came the fences
  closing out the rest of the world.

Then came the refugees
  Jews from neighboring villages and countryside
  weighed down with wagons of belongings
  herded inside the wire
with no houses in which to live.

Then came the other family
  assigned to share our home.
Ten people
  six in my family
  four in the other
crammed in a three-room house.

Then came the confiscations
   anything of value
      jewelry
      money
even Mama and Tata's wedding bands.

Then came the shortages of
   food
   water
   medicine
   jobs
   coal
   firewood.

I was fortunate.
Even though
school was forbidden,
at seventeen
I had a job outside the ghetto
   at a small bank
where people hated me
   because I was smart
   spoke different languages
      Polish
      Russian
      German
   was a Jew.

Then
   even that was taken away.

You cannot work here anymore,
   I was told.
No Jews.
Oleg Broz's father smiled
as I walked out.

Then
came
the
transports.

The List

The *Judenrat* ran the ghetto
  enforced the Nazis' laws.
They posted lists
  names of families
to be sent away.
No rhyme or reason.
Just a list of names.

I checked the list
every night on my way home
from scrounging food
  trading through the barbed-wire fence
      shoes
      dresses
      books
  for a bag of flour
      potatoes
      meat
  with Poles
      some of whom wanted to help
      some of whom were nearly as desperate as we
      some of whom wanted everything.

A tattered paper tacked to
the synagogue door.
I avoided neighbors' faces
too embarrassed to see

naked fear
or relief.

The first day
    our name was not on the list.
Relief
    of not being sent away.
The second day
    our name was not on the list.
Fear
    of what was yet to come.

The third day
    my eyes tripped down the list.

Scarf tightened.
Breath stopped.
Head spun.
I blinked.
My heart climbed up my throat
    along with what little food was in my stomach.
Cold sweat dripped down my spine.
I forced myself to
    look again.

No mistake.
No mirage.
Sznaiderhauz.
My name.

My family.

The third day.
Terror
  of the unknown.

Family Decisions

Partisans hid in the countryside
   fighting against the Germans.
Iser wanted to join them.
Mama would hear none of it.
You are just a boy,
   she said, cradling his face in her shaking hands.

But, Mama!
   Iser's voice cracked
   his face flushed.

We must stay together,
   Tata decided.
We must do as we are told.
We have done nothing wrong.
We have nothing to fear.
The Germans are not monsters.

I could not imagine Iser
a partisan,
   fighting
   in the woods
   against the Germans.
He was just a boy,
   my little brother,
even if he had grown taller
in the year since his bar mitzvah.

I could not imagine myself
a partisan,
  fighting
  in the woods
  against the Germans.
I was just a girl
  yet I wanted to go.
Wanted to fight,
do something other than
what I was told.

Little Lázaro played happily
  oblivious
on the floor with his train.
Smiling when the wheels spun
round so fast they hummed.

Necha's head bowed over a book
  oblivious also,
    though she was old enough
    to know better,
her feet tucked under her
to keep them warm.

But, Tata,
    Iser argued.
But, Tata,
    I argued.
Tata cut us both off with
a stern look.
Enough, Iser.
Zlatka, mind yourself,
    Tata's voice harder than I had ever heard.
No more discussion.

I knew
    even if he disagreed with Tata
Iser would do as he was told.
I wondered,
    If I were a boy,
    would I?

It Would Have Been Enough

If God had allowed us to stay
    in our own home
Dayenu
It would have been enough.

If God had allowed us
    to take in refugees
Dayenu
It would have been enough.

If God had provided wood
    to heat our home
Dayenu
It would have been enough.

If God had given me
    a job outside the ghetto
Dayenu
It would have been enough.

If God had given us
    enough to eat
Dayenu
It would have been enough.

If God had kept our names
    off the transport list for two days

Dayenu
It would have been enough.

If God had kept us all together
Dayenu
It would have been enough.

But I wondered,
   Was it?

Worldly Possessions

The *Judenrat* told us,
  Bring only what you can carry.
  Only what is necessary.

What do I pack?
  Mama fretted.
Only what is necessary,
  Tata answered.
But what is necessary?
  Mama's voice rose.
We don't know where we are going.
We don't know how long we will be gone.
Just take,
  Tata said,
what you cannot live without.

A change of clothes.
Something nice
  for *Shabbos.*
Wool sweaters
overcoats
  to keep us warm.
A silver frame
  to hold the family together.
Shabbos candlesticks
  wrapped in Mama's undergarments.

Tata's *Torah* and *Talmud*
    tucked under his suit.

Iser's *tallis* and *tefillin*
    gifts for becoming bar mitzvah.
    Such a good boy and a better man, Mama said.

Necha's well-worn book
    read a dozen times.
    You will go blind you read so much, Mama said.

The engine to Lázaro's train set
    with wheels that spun.
    It's so heavy, Mama said.

I looked about
    the home where I was reared
    the home we all loved.
    But what about . . . ?

These are just things, Zlatka,
    Tata said.
Things can be replaced.
As long as we are together
we will be home.
    Tata kissed my forehead.
No matter what comes,
the spark of God

resides inside you
  in us all.
No one can take that.

That night
  even though it wasn't *Shabbos*
Tata wrapped his arms around
  Iser
  Necha
  Lázaro
  and me
and whispered a blessing,
May God bless you and keep you.
May God shine His face upon you
  and grant you graciousness.
May God's presence be with you
  and grant you peace.

In the morning
I packed what I could not live without
  a pad of paper and colored pencils,
  a strand of paper soldiers, precisely cut
  to entertain Lázaro.
Such a hobby for a smart girl, Mama said.

Our worldly possessions,
  in three small cardboard suitcases.

All Aboard!

Mama locked the door
  one last time.
Tucked the key inside
her best handbag
  the one she used on *Shabbos*.

Tata led
  a suitcase in one hand
  a food hamper
      carefully packed
  in the other.
Following the migrating stream
to the train station.
Not meeting the gaze
of anyone on the street.

We waited.
The Sznaiderhauz family
with hundreds of other families
  quietly, orderly
clutching possessions
clutching each other.
Doing as they were told,
for they refused to believe
that anything horrible
could happen to them.

But life had changed.
I'd seen hatred in the eyes of
   classmates
   teachers
   villagers
   coworkers
   customers
   Oleg Broz.
Anything could happen.

German soldiers
   with guns
shouldered between the crowd,
prying clutching arms apart
separating families
separating the men.

Lázaro cried.
Necha sobbed.

Someone shouted.
Someone pushed.
Heads turned.
A group of boys
   my age or Iser's
ran for the fence.

Some ducked under
and bolted for the woods.

Iser twitched beside me.
I gripped his shoulder
   grounding him to the family
   to me.

Soldiers pursued
   shooting
mowing down the boys
leaving them in the dirt
   like weeds.

Glances exchanged
between
Mama and Tata
   as the men were led away.
No words.
Not even an embrace.
Their eyes said
what their mouths could not
   for fear of scaring us children
   for fear of terrifying themselves.

Iser
as he followed Tata
determined to be a man

the man Mama promised
he'd become.

Iser would survive.

I had to believe that
otherwise the Germans won.

The Train

rumbled onward.
Through the one high
window I saw
a white winter
sky streaked with dark
black smoke, and snow
falling wet and
heavy like tears.
Sounds came only
from the steel wheels
screaming, cold wind
whistling, and the
boxcars groaning.
Inside, muted
whimpers. Necha
had whined to the
point where I had
thought I might strike
her to make her
hush up. We all
wanted to cry.
Most of us had.
But not me. No!
I would not show
my fear, terror,
sorrow to the
Germans. I would

show them   I was
stronger   than they
supposed   a girl—
a Jew—   could be,
        should be.

Inside

The first time
I ever took a train
it had been to Warsaw.

Out of all the students
   in my whole school
I'd won the prize!
I had been the best.
Smarter than all the boys
   all the Gentiles.
Even Oleg Broz.
To be recognized
   rewarded
A girl.
A Jew.
It was, I'd told Mama,
As if I'd touched heaven.

Mama, Tata,
   Iser, Necha, and Lázaro
had waved
from the platform.
Faces flushed with pride.
Iser's jaw set,
   as if he were determined to win
   when he got the chance.

Far from first class
    still, I'd had a wicker seat.
The parcel of food
    Mama had packed
    in my lap
        a cold knish stuffed with
                potato
                onion
                liver
        a slice of honey cake stuffed with
                moisture
                sweetness
                memories.

This train ride was different.

The train rumbled.
People pressed inside
    like a flower from a boy
    flattened inside a book.
So close we breathed
    the same stagnant air.
So close our thoughts collided
    eyes wide
    faces pale
    lips chewed.

Lázaro's
    head against Mama's leg
    eyes closed
    thumb at his mouth,
    long gone the paper soldiers
    I had cut for him.
Necha's
    head on my shoulder
    the slow and steady
    breath of sleep,
    her whining finally silenced
    by exhaustion.
Mama's
    head upright
    eyes bright with tears
    no false smile
    for Necha and Lázaro,
    no more need for pretending.
My own head
    almost too heavy to hold
    held on to memories
    the spark of God,
    dreamt of the horizon.

This train ride was different.

Why Is This Different?

At every Passover seder we ask
  Mah nishtanoh?
  Why is this different?
Memories of rituals and celebrations
  unbidden
  yet welcome.

So much preparation
  Necha
  dragged from reading,
  me
  torn from drawing
to help Mama.

Holidays begin at sundown.
The night before
Tata hid ten slices of bread
  about the house
chametz we were sure to find.

Iser led the search,
  candle in hand
  to see in all the corners.
Lázaro, the feather
  to sweep away the crumbs.
Necha, the wooden spoon
  to hold all we found.

I, the paper bag
    to carry it all away.
A somber business
    done with smiling faces.

The following morning
Tata built a fire
    chametz floated away
    in smoke.
The house clean.
Our hearts purged.

Dressed in our best.
When we were little,
Necha and I dressed up
in Mama's clothes
    pretending
    wishing
to be grown.

The table set
with the best dishes
    seder plate
            bitter herbs
            greens for dipping
            shank bone
            hard boiled egg
            charoset
    matzoh

candlesticks
wine cups
    filled with
    sweetness
    even for us children.

Lázaro asking
the Four Questions
    Mah nishtanoh?
    Why is this different?

The search for the *afikomen*.
Giggles.
Smiles.
Laughter.
Love.

Singing
  songs
  blessings.

Next year in Jerusalem!

But *mah nishtanoh?*
This year was different.

Icicles

Boxcar window
  with no glass or shutter
winter wind rushed in.
Cold.
Fresh.
A mixed blessing.

Outside
  an icicle.
I reached high.
Stood on tiptoes
  stretched.
So cold it burned.
So cold it brought revival.

A lick for Lázaro.
A slurp for Necha.
Pass it to Mama,
  I told my sister, who held on for one more taste.
You first, Zlatka, Mama said.

Delicious.
Cold.
Wet.
Like ice cream on a summer's day,
  gone too soon.
Leaving lips slick with its memory.

The Toilet

A bucket.
In the corner.
Full to overflowing.
Eyes watered.
Stomachs roiled.
Gags swallowed.
I turned away
   granting
a semblance of privacy.

Stopping

Once a day the train stopped.
Groaning, squealing, jostling.
I braced myself
   as best I could
against Necha and
the women pressed behind me.
But like dominoes
we fell
into the filth on the floor.

Doors flew open,
   bright sunshine stabbed my eyes.
Soldiers yelled,
     Mach schnell! Mach schnell!
    Make it quick! Make it quick!

I brushed what I could
from my clothes,
shuffled on stiff, numb legs
to the door,
held Necha's hand.
Mama and Lázaro behind.

I jumped
onto the cold, hard ground,
   my knees and jaw jarring

helped Necha
and Lázaro.
Mama fell
    slipped or was pushed.
Palms and chin
scraped and bloodied.

Dogs snarled
    teeth bared.
SS yelled
    guns ready.

Clean, cold air
washed away the stench
reminded me of home.

Bodies
    taken from the train
    left in a pile
like garbage.

I turned Lázaro away.
Pointed to a murder of crows
    gathering in the sky
    like a black storm cloud.

Mach schnell!
A line,
 chunks of stale bread.
I'm hungry, Mama,
 Lázaro said.
Take mine, tateleh.
I shared my portion
with Necha.

Another bucket filled with dirty water.
A ladle shared by all.
Don't drink the water,
 I said,
scooping snow from the ground.
Necha did not listen.

Bad Water

A rush for the bucket.
Tears streaked Necha's face
  as filth streaked her legs.
She was not alone.
Too many for a single bucket.
I broke off another icicle.
Here, drink this.

Chapter 2

Fania

Belief in God?

Why did I still
Believe in God
When I felt so
Godforsaken?

Maybe
It had been
All those hours
By Leybl's side
As he prepared
For his
Bar mitzvah.
Mushke,
Just a little girl then,
Four years younger than I,
Played with her dolls
While I sat,
Like an uncooked
Matzoh ball,

Beside my older brother.
Absorbing his learning,
Swelling,
With knowledge
And understanding.

I'd never asked
If I could study also.
Learning
Was for boys.
I was a good girl.

We worshipped
Education,
Schools,
Books,
Newspapers,
Debates,
Rather than
Torah
And *Talmud*.

Still,
Every Friday night
Papa said *Kiddush*
To bless the wine
And Mama lit candles.

Holidays were spent
With family—
Aunts, uncles,
Cousins.
The whole
Mishpocheh,
Family from near and far.

I'd learned
Watching Leybl,
How to pray.
How to ask *Adonai* for
Forgiveness,
Peace,
Understanding,
Help.

But *Adonai* had not
Answered my prayers
For a long,
Long,
Long
Time.

Białystok

God did not
Answer my prayers
When the Germans
Came,
Like a swarm of locusts,
To Białystok.

Once a thriving city,
More Jewish than Polish,
With Yiddish theaters,
Schools,
Newspapers.

We'd lived happily
In a ghetto
Of our own making
Surrounded by Jews.

Within a month
Of the Germans' arrival,
We were fenced in
With no food.
No money.
Sharing a two-room apartment
With two old ladies
We did not know.
With two thin mattresses

To share between the five of us.
Papa,
Mama,
Mushke,
Me,
And Leybl on the hard wooden floor.

Mushke complained
When Leybl snored.
Hush, hush,
   Mama said.
He needs his sleep.
Mushke and I needed sleep too,
But I stayed quiet,
Like Mama said.

Papa and Leybl
Worked at night
At a factory
In the ghetto,
Cleaning up after the workers
Had left for the day.
I worked
Outside the ghetto
Cleaning,
Washing floors,
Scrubbing toilets.
I did what I was told.

I sewed patches
On our sleeves.
Yellow equilateral triangles,
Stars of David.
Pricking my finger
With every stitch.

We lived miserably
In a ghetto
Not of our own making
Surrounded by Nazis.

Yet I thanked God
For keeping us
All together.

The First *Aktion*

It was in February.
The sun had not yet cracked
The horizon.
Papa and Leybl
Were working the night shift.
Mama, Mushke, and I
Slept.

It was the sound of footsteps
Trying to be silent—
But hundreds of soldiers
Moving through the streets
Cannot be quiet—
That woke me.

It was Mama who said,
To the basement,
And shooed Mushke and me
Down the rickety steps
To the damp stone basement
Where even Mushke had to duck
So as not to hit her head.

It was the begging
That frightened me
More than the gunshots
Or the screams,

Even more than the tread of
Heavy boots on the floors
Above us.

It was the begging
Of husbands,
Wives,
Mothers,
Fathers
That was not heard
By the soldiers,
Or by God,
But was heard by
Mama,
Mushke,
And me
As we cowered in the corner
Of the basement.

It was dark again
When Mama sent me to find Papa
And Leybl.
I did not want to go.
Still, I climbed the rickety steps
Only to rush back down and beg
Mama to let me stay.

Please, Fania. Be a good girl,
She said,
And sent me up again.

It was the stench of blood,
Bodies,
Gun smoke,
Death
That filled the cold winter's night air.

It was the frozen stares,
Open eyes,
White faces,
Broken bodies
Crumpled on the cobblestone street.

It was the crows,
Human scavengers,
Pecking at the bodies,
Searching for a loved one,
A morsel of food,
Something of value
That made my footsteps quicken,
Stepping over corpses
To find if my loved ones
Were still alive.

Searching

I made it all the way
To the factory
Without finding
Papa or Leybl
Or their bodies.

Polish soldiers
Stood outside the factory doors
And I was too terrified
Of the soldiers,
Of the truth,
To ask
If Papa and Leybl
Were still inside,
Still alive.

I headed home,
Knowing Mama
Would be angry,
Would die of fright,
Wondering
What had happened to
Papa and Leybl.
Disappointed
I had no answers for her.

Voices,
Warm and welcoming,
Met me at the door.
Arms,
Strong and supporting,
Surrounded me.
Cheeks,
Scratchy yet soft,
Pressed against my face.

Papa and Leybl!
Hid in the factory's basement,
Like Mama, Mushke, and I
Hid in the apartment basement.
I'd passed them
In the dark,
In the horror,
Never knowing
They searched for us,
Like I searched for them.

Disbelief

Mama and Papa
Were naive.
Even after the *Aktion*,
All they'd seen,
All that death,
They still couldn't believe.

The Germans are a civilized people,
Papa said.
Bach, Beethoven, and Wagner
Were German,
Mama said.
And Goethe, Nietzsche, and Karl Marx,
Papa said,
How could such a society
Produce such masters
And such monsters?

Still,
Mama said in a whisper,
We must protect Leybl.

Papa nodded.
The rest of us are safe,
They won't hurt women, children, or old men like me,
But Leybl is young, smart, strong.
We must protect Leybl.

Not as sure as Papa and Mama,
I wondered,
Who would protect
Mushke and me?
But I did not ask.

Leaving Białystok

In late summer,
A friend of Papa's
Had two passes to travel to Augustów,
The countryside
Where it was *Judenfrei*,
Cleansed of Jews,
Where we could find
A place
For Leybl to hide.

Leybl couldn't show his face.
Papa would never leave Mama.
Mama would never leave Papa.
Mushke was just a little girl.

Fania,
Mama said,
Looks the most Aryan.
Mama said,
She will be safe.
She is a good girl.
No one will suspect.

I never doubted her.

In Augustów
I took off my patches,

The yellow Stars of David,
And whispered prayers
To give me strength,
To help me find a safe haven for Leybl,
To keep me safe,
And wore a pretty white dress,
Just like all the Gentile girls.

My heart climbed into my throat
I was not like all the Gentile girls
I am a Jew.

Found Out

I had not gone far,
No more than fifteen feet.

A young boy,
Younger than Mushke,
Pointed at me.
She is a Jew,
He said.

I laughed,
But people stopped and stared.
I denied,
But he said it again,
She is a Jew.
I tried to walk on,
But the crowd did not let me.
I laughed,
Again,
But a policeman arrived
And then a German soldier.

It did not matter
That I looked like
All the other Polish girls
Without my yellow armband.

It did not matter
That I'd whispered prayers
To *Adonai*
To keep me safe.

Papa's friend stood
On the other side of the street
Watching
As I was hauled away.
He did not claim me.
I did not claim him.
I had been told not to.

She is a Jew.
She is a Jew.

Łomża Prison

I was sent to
The prison in Łomża,
Held with other Jewish girls
Rounded up from areas
Supposedly *Judenfrei*.

Seven of us
Jammed in a cell
Big enough for one.
A girl with blond braids
And a gold cross
Got down on her knees,
Crossed herself,
And swore to God
She was not a Jew.
No one listened
Not even God.

Days spent in
A cramped cell,
No room to lie down,
No information,
No food.
Worries for my family
Chewed at my heart,
Mice in the corners
Of the cell.

I heard rumors.
Białystok ghetto
Was liquidated,
Emptied,
Destroyed,
Burned.
Most had done as they were told,
Climbed onto trains.
Others had fought.

Mama,
Papa,
Mushke
Would not have fought.

Leybl?
What would my brother have done?

I prayed
He'd climbed on a train.
The rumors claimed
No one survived
The uprising.

God Knows

How long I stayed in Łomża.

One day,
Without warning
We were loaded into boxcars.
Even the girl with blond braids
Who swore she was not a Jew.

We were told
We were being taken to
A clean camp
With less crowding
And more food.

As the train gained speed
The girl with blond braids
Squeezed herself through
The one high window
And threw herself from
The moving train.

Only God knows now
If she was a Jew
Or not.

Stutthof

We arrived in Stutthof
In the middle of the night
With the wind blowing off
The Baltic Sea.
Too far away to smell the salt
But close enough to feel wisps of cooler air.

Once sorted
And selected,
I asked anyone
Who would listen,
Are you from Białystok?
Some nodded.
Do you know my family?
My papa?
Yankl Landau?
My mama?
Sore Landau?
My sister?
Mushke?
My brother?
Leybl?
Heads shook
Eyes lowered.

The girls from Łomża
Bronia,

Guta,
Giza,
Stayed by my side
When my heart crumpled,
A piece of paper discarded.

Another Transport

During the months in Stutthof
I still prayed,
Asking *Adonai*
For understanding,
Strength,
Help.
If I was a good girl,
Adonai would hear me.

As we were loaded
Onto another train,
I asked,
Is my family alive?
Where are we going?
But there was no answer.

Only rumors.
The name
Auschwitz
Rumbled like train wheels
Through the boxcar.

And I prayed some more
That that was not so,
For I had heard

More rumors.

Chapter 3

Zlatka

Disembarking

Once again, the train stopped.
Groaning, squealing, jostling.
I didn't know
  how many days
      stops
      deaths
there had been.
It had become routine.
I held Necha close,
leaned against the wall
so we didn't fall.

Doors flew open.
I closed my eyes
  against
bright sunshine.
Soldiers yelled,
    Mach schnell! Mach schnell!

We jumped
  fell
  were pushed
from the train.
Human cargo disgorged.

The SS waited
  guns ready
  dogs barking
on the *Judenrampe*
  between the trains.

Hundreds of people.
Faces haunted
  confused
  frightened
  defiant.
Clutching cardboard suitcases
  leather satchels
  canvas bags
each other.
Not just a stop
a final destination.

The name
  Auschwitz
rippled through the chaos
but it meant nothing—
  yet.

Mama rose to tiptoes
  scanning the crowd
looking for Tata and Iser.
All around
women hunted for a husband,
                    father,
                    brother,
                        son.
Little children clung to coat hems.

Do you see them?
  I asked.
Mama shook her head.
  You try.

I lifted my chin
scanned
  above the crowds.
No Tata.
No Iser.
Fences.
Everywhere fences
  too high to climb
hummed with electricity.

Men in striped uniforms
  gaunt and stooped
  yellow stars

loaded corpses
   dumped from the train
onto handcarts.
Their eyes ringed dark
   as if they'd looked
   too often
   into Death's eyes.

Nearby chimneys
belched black smoke
into clear blue skies.
A sweet stench
turned my empty stomach.

Selection

Mach schnell!
Herded into line.
Staying close together.
Mama led the way,
    Lázaro at her hip,
    Necha's left hand on his shoulder,
    Necha's right hand glued to mine.

Divided.
    To the left.
    Frail
    Older
    Younger
    Sick

                                                  To the right.
                                                       Robust
                                                        Young
                                                      Healthy
                                                       Strong

Mama's eyes locked on mine.
Words unspoken.

Mama knew.
Take care of your sister.

I knew.
I will.

Where are we going, Mama?
  Lázaro asked.
Mama smiled.
My eyes stung.
How could she smile?
How could she be so brave?
You and I are going to meet Tata and Iser,
  she said.
Necha pulled against my embrace.
I want to see Tata and Iser too.
No, Mama's voice like cold wind.
Stay with Zlatka.

Mama's arms around us all.
A whispered blessing,
  May God bless you and keep you.
  May God shine His face upon you
    and grant you graciousness.
  May God's presence be with you
    and grant you peace.

Those words,
same words
whispered by Tata every *Shabbos*.

A soldier between us.

Mama and Lázaro to the left.

                        Necha and I to the right.

                    Mama! Necha screamed.
                          Come, Necha.
                  I led my sister away
                     my voice calm
         as if someone else were speaking.

Stories

I had heard.
Word had gotten out
   it floated through the Polish countryside
   carried on the wind.
After the Russians fled
   and before the Germans first arrived.

Rumors
Of camps with barbed wire
   and electrified fences.
Of starvation and work.
Of showers with no water.
Of giant furnaces that burned all day.

But I did not believe.
No one believed.
Stories.
Warnings.
Truth.
Brought by Russians
   partisans
   a few who had escaped.

People knew.
People didn't,
        wouldn't,
                couldn't
believe.

Quiet Dignity

Over my shoulder
I watched
Mama and Lázaro
walk away.

Mama's head high
  back straight.
Her arm around Lázaro's shoulder
  as she leaned over to say something to him.

Her words floated back
  a small gift from God.

Say the Shema *with me.*
  Hear, O Israel: the Lord is our God, the Lord is One.
  Blessed be the Name of His glorious kingdom for ever and ever.

Lázaro did as Mama told him.

Necha struggled,
  cried
to join Mama and Lázaro.
I held tight.

Only Two

I only had Necha.
Necha only had me.

My sister crumpled to the ground
  a grieving heap.
Soldiers stared at us.
I pulled Necha
  onto her feet
  pushed her forward
so Necha would not be
taken too.

Chapter 4

Fania

Showers

Hundreds of girls pushed forward.
Led into the *Sauna.*
Take off your clothes!
Those who asked, *Why?*
Regretted it.
I remained quiet.
Arms crossed,
Covered what I could
From soldiers' stares.

I'd lost my white dress
Long ago
And had no possessions,
But another transport
Arrived the same time
Mixing those of us from Stutthof
With women and girls,
Fresh from home,

Who gently placed
Their worldly possessions
On benches,
Hung their dresses
On pegs in the wall
As if to reclaim them.

I didn't know
What was happening,
What would happen,
But I knew enough
To know
They'd never see
Their belongings,
Dresses,
Hats,
Scarves,
Handbags
Again.
But it hurt
My heart
Too much
To tell them.

Abandoned in a pile
Clothing,
Shoes,
Jewelry,

Suitcases,
Books,
Drawing paper and colored pencils.

Scissors,
Cold against my scalp.
Shorn hair drifted
To the floor.
Riding crops whistled through the air.
Lashed against bare skin.
Screams bounced off
The tiled walls.

Mach schnell!
We rushed forward
To avoid the beatings.
We rushed backward
To avoid the beatings.
Mach schnell!

What had we done
To deserve such abuse?

In the room of naked women,
Holding hands
With the girls from Łomża,
I'd never felt so
Alone.

Above the noise
A voice called,
Necha?
Worried.
Brave, since any sound brought down the riding crop.

Doused with cold water.
Scrubbed with lye soap
Rough against my skin,
Stung my eyes.

The voice again
Necha?
Frightened.

Mach schnell!
A riding crop to the back,
The face,
The legs.

Another girl,
Her eyes wild with more than fear
Fell to the floor
Laughing.
Taken away.
Not even covered before they dragged her outside.

The voice again,
Necha! Where is Necha?

Panicked.
Joined by a second voice,
Zlatka?

Necha was younger,
Though not as young as Mushke.
Thinner,
Frailer,
Already.

Zlatka about my age.
Capable,
Stronger,
Already.

Sisters.
Family resemblance
Obvious
Despite their bald heads.

I had to tuck thoughts
Of Mushke
Away.

Necha,
The younger one,
Laughed.
Teetered to the edge of madness.
Zlatka,

The older sister,
Shook Necha's shoulders
Until she looked into her eyes.
Then Zlatka said,
You look like Lázaro.
Her voice strong, but playful.
You look like Iser,
Necha said.

They both laughed
Until other women stepped away
Until riding crops were raised.

Still,
I watched,
Missing Mushke.
Laughter,
Not of the mad
But of the living.

Processing

We pushed forward.
Zlatka and Necha in front of me.
The girls from Łomża behind.

No talking,
A girl
At a table writing names,
Wearing the striped uniform,
Speaking Yiddish,
Working for the Germans,
Whispered.

Family name?
Landau.
First name?
Fania.
The girl wrote,
Waved her hand,
Dismissed me.
A bothersome bug.

Another girl dipped a pen in ink
Then jabbed it
Under the skin.
Painful
Puncture
After

Painful
Puncture.
Tattooed numbers
On Necha's and Zlatka's forearms.
Necha cried.
Zlatka didn't.

I turned away
When it was my turn.
Each stab
Each drop of ink
Pierced my crumpled paper heart.

Underwear.
Slip.
A *shmatte*,
To cover my head
Tied rough under my chin.
Striped dresses.
Too big for me,
Too small for others.
Sleeves drooped over my hands,
Like Mushke dressing up in Mama's clothes.

More patches,
Two yellow triangles
For most of us.
Others with
Different-colored triangles

Stood apart,
As if they were better.

Soon we would learn
That, in Auschwitz,
They were.

Wooden shoes,
Too large,
Clomped on the floor.

I stumbled forward,
Wished for my white dress.
Though it had not saved me,
At least it had been pretty.

Products off an assembly line.
Blood and ink dripped
From our left forearms.

Rules

Mama's good girl
Followed the rules.
At home.
At school.
In synagogue.
Even when the Germans came.
With signs that read:
JUDEN VERBOTEN,
Jews Forbidden.
I did as I was told.

But in a world
Where girls were tattooed
With numbers.
And bodies were tossed away
Like garbage.

There were no rules.

Hierarchy

Nazis believed
In a master race,
An Aryan race,
Better than everyone else.

Jews
Were
Subhuman.

In Auschwitz,
Black Triangles,
Vagrants and prostitutes,
Green Triangles,
Criminals,
Tended to agree.

New rules.

In Auschwitz,
Yellow Triangles,
Jews,
Were the majority.
But Jews
Were given
The smallest,
Poorest
Portions,

The hardest,
Most grueling
Work,
The least attentive,
Effective
Medical care,
The toughest,
Deadliest
Beatings.

Jews
Were the least likely
To survive.

Head to Toe

We were herded in *Blocks*,
Barracks, originally built as stables.
Each *Block*
Divided into eighteen *Stuben*,
Stalls, to house the horses.
Two *Stuben*,
At the far end,
For necessary buckets.
In each of the sixteen remaining *Stuben* was one,
Sometimes two, *Kojen*,
Three-tiered bunk beds.

In our bunk,
The girls from Łomża and I
Slept with two others.
Front to back
And head to toe.
There were eight girls
In the bunk above us,
And seven below us.

No one slept that night.

Birkenau Math

I was not particularly good at math.
But I could not help counting.

Approximately:
7 x 3 = 21 girls per *Koje*.
21 x 1.2 = 25.2 girls per *Stube*.
25.2 x 16 = 403.2 girls per *Block*.

There were twenty *Blocks* in each row.
403.2 x 20 = 8,064 girls per row.
Nine rows of *Blocks*.
8,064 x 9 = 72,576 girls in our section.

Through the barbed-wire fence,
More sections.
Rows and rows
Of more *Blocks*.
Some made of brick.
Some made of wood.
Some two stories.
Some one.

Not even God could count that high.

Animals

Transported like cattle.
Shorn like sheep.
Branded like livestock.
Housed in a stable.

Tower of Babel

Whispers filled the night air.
Polish.
German.
French.
Czech.
Russian.
Hebrew.
Yiddish.
Hungarian.
Dutch.
Greek.
Slovak.

Chapter 5

Zlatka

Triangles

Black   Asocial

Green Habitual criminal

Red   Political prisoner

Blue   Emigrant

Pink   Homosexual

Violet   Jehovah's Witness

Brown   Gypsy

Yellow   Jew

Yellow Triangles

Yellow

triangles   were   considered

beneath   all   the

others.

The First Night

Inside *Block* number 19
stench worse than the boxcars.
A *Koje* near a window,
I pushed Necha to the top
  the window sealed shut
but I could still see the horizon.

Four more girls beside us.
Front to back,
front to back,
front to back.
Necha's shoulders shook.

Squished between the wall and Necha
  out the sealed window
past the ditch
  filled with slime,
the electrified fence
  with a sign
  ACHTUNG! LEBENSGEFAHR!
  Attention! Danger!
I could see the horizon.

Stark shades from black to white
memories
  of sunsets
  filled with colors

memories
  Tata told me
  to hold inside.

I lay as still as darkness.
More color in me
than the yellow of my patches.

Prayers

The *Shema*
   daily declaration of faith
recited according to Deuteronomy
      "When you lie down and when you rise up"
   regardless of age or gender.

Then *Kaddish*
   the prayer for the dead
only recited by a *minyan*
   ten male Jews past the age of *bar mitzvah*.
But I whispered it
   even though there was no *minyan*
   even though I was a girl
for Mama and Lázaro
   not for Tata and Iser
   not yet.

Prayers floated between my lips,
   above the *Koje*,
         over the *Stube* walls,
               to the ceiling of the *Block*.

Gathered together
   like cobwebs
in the rafters.

Food

The *blockova*
  picked by the Germans
  to keep order in the *Blocks*
handed out
one bowl
one spoon.

Prized possessions
when everything else had been taken.

Keep them with you always.
Otherwise they would be stolen,
  by those who had lost their own
  by those who bartered for more.

Breakfast.
Brown water
called coffee.

Necha whined,
  It's cold.

It's just right,
  I said.
You won't burn your mouth.

Dinner.
Dingy water
called soup.

Necha pushed forward
to be among the first in line.

Wait.
   I held her back.
Those first in line
get only broth.
If we're at the end of the line
maybe we'll get a chunk of potato,
   an onion,
   or even, praise Adonai,
   a piece of meat
   that has sunk to the bottom.

A chunk of brown bread
a pat of margarine.
To be saved for morning.
I picked out the weevils
and ate it all.

Who knew what would happen
   between dinner and morning?

Quarantine

Week after week.
Of nothing.
Sitting.
Outside.
In the snow.
Waiting.

For the first month
our group was separated from the others.
A prison within a prison.
Allowing time
   fear
   fatigue
to do what the Selections
had not.

Some girls went mad
   laughter that was not merry.
Others stopped caring
   hunger that turned to starvation.

Necha folded in on herself.
I'm tired,
   she said.
I forced her
   dragged her
   cajoled her

to walk around the yard.
We must keep strong.
It will keep you warm.
If you walk with me,
   I'll share my bread with you.

Each week
   fewer of us remained.

Waiting.
In the snow.
Outside.
Sitting.
For nothing.
Week after week.

Roll Call

Appell.
Every morning.
Shivering in the snow.
Precise rows of five.
Standing still as they counted
tattoos.

Necha swayed.
I had warned her,
  Don't drink that water.
I'm thirsty. I'm hungry;
  Necha hadn't listened.

Counted.
Recounted.
Corpses dragged from the *Kojen.*
Hours later counted again.
Appell ended.

Necha collapsed.

A mother with two daughters
  moved away.
Four girls
  I'd seen during processing
watched.
One, with a kind smile,

Fania, I thought her name was,
stepped forward
but backed away
when the *blockova* asked,

Is she sick?
No, just a little tired,
    I answered.
It's Block 25 for her if she doesn't get better.
I pulled Necha to her feet.
No! No! She's okay. Look, she's fine.
I smiled
    the smile Mama had given Lázaro.

The *blockova* turned away.

Fania and the three girls watched,
    not smiling.
On Fania's face
    the truth.

I turned away.

Illness

Anger
    at Necha for drinking the foul water
    at myself for not stopping her.

Snow
    to wash away the filth
    to cool her burning fever.

Wished
    I could cut out paper dolls to distract her
    I could do more than worry.

Worried
    that Necha would not get better
    that the *blockova* would notice.

Hurried
    to trade coffee for a bit of bread
    to find some help.

Returned
    Necha wasn't there
    Necha wasn't anywhere.

Frantic
    I raced around the *Block*
    I searched everywhere.

Others
    the mother with the two daughters turned away
    Fania and the other girls shook their heads.

Guilt
    I had left her alone
    I had not taken care of her.

Waited
    all day alone
    all day knowing.

Block 25

Necha did not return
  that night
  or
  in the morning.

Where is my sister?

The *blockova*'s ice-blue eyes danced
her thin-lipped smile curled.
To Block *25*.

Too late, I ran
  to catch up to Necha
  to catch up to death.

Circling *Block* 25
  for some way out
  for some way in.

Black-booted SS laughed
  shoved me away.

Bile rose in my throat.
Hollowness swelled in my heart.

Despair

Unfamiliar faces all around.
Cold shoulders against my back at night.
Someone stole my spot against the wall
  stole my view of the horizon.

No mother to talk to.
No brother to play with.
No sister to laugh with.

My heart hardened
  cold
    as death.

Stuck in the Mud

Standing in *Appell*.
Waiting for the counting.

Barely aware of
gray-red mud seeping
around my wooden shoes
   over my feet,
        tugging at my ankles.

A *Kapo* walked through the group
  pointing,
      pointing,
           pointing.
Selecting for a *Kommando*
  work squad.

You.
You.
You.

Five more times.

Then at me.

Mach schnell!
Always a rush.

But the gray-red mud held tight.

Death's grasp around my foot.
I pulled.
My foot slipped
the shoe did not.

I would die
    in the *Kommando* without a shoe
I would die
    in the gray-red mud of Birkenau.

For the first time
since we'd been rounded
into the ghetto,
my cold, hard heart
did not care
if I lived or died.

Death would bring a reunion
    with Mama
    Lázaro
    Necha.

Hold still,
a Yiddish whisper
    as someone's hands dug around my foot.

An unfamiliar face.
Another You.

Free from the gray-red mud.

We marched behind the *Kapo*.

To Work

Through the gates of Birkenau.
Through the countryside.
No billowing smoke.
No rancid smells.
Clean air.
Cold air.
Horizon filled with color.

But for the soldiers
   with their guns
   and angry shouts.
But for the dogs
   with their teeth
   and growling snarls.
But for the Aryan girls
   Black Triangles
   prisoners like us
       but not like us
   with their clenched fists
   and hate-filled eyes.

Nine of us
   trod through the forest
   apart from the others
   waited for the beatings
      whippings
         death.

Move those rocks.
A riding crop cut through the air
   sliced a back.

I worked alongside the girl who saved my shoe.
I am Eta.
Small, like Necha.
Young, like Necha.
But brimming with anger,
   like me.

For hours we moved rocks.
Nine Jewish girls
   wrestled with boulders
       Jacob wrestling with the angel.
The Aryan girls flirted with the soldiers,
   disappeared into the woods
       two by two
       like Noah's ark
   he returned with a smile
   and she with a cigarette.

An extra meal for *Aussenkommandos*
   for hard labor outside camp.
Soldiers passed out bread.
First to the Aryan girls.
Smallest pieces
   for us Jewish girls.

I chewed my bread
  moldy and hard
  as my anger
  as my heart.
I bit my tongue.

Eta did not.

Eyes lowered
  hands clasped before her.
Eta spoke just above a whisper
  in German
  to a boy in uniform
  who looked no older than she
  who might have smiled at her
  on a street in Berlin
  just a year or two ago.

His anger was harder than the crust of bread
  harder than the boulders
  harder than his fists.

Eta collapsed.

Jackboots stomped.
Fists clobbered.
Riding crops whipped.
Rifle butts smashed.
Billy clubs crushed.

Then the dogs.

I watched
   teeth biting lips
      until I tasted copper
   bread churning stomach
      until I lost what I had eaten.

Back to work!

For hours we moved rocks.
Eight Jewish girls
   wrestled with boulders
      Israel wrestling with God.
The Aryan girls flirted with the soldiers,
   disappeared into the woods
      two by two
      like Noah's ark
   he returned with a smile
   and she with a cigarette.

Eight of us
   trod through the forest
   apart from the others
   taking turns
      carrying Eta.

Even the dead needed to be counted at *Appell.*

Echoes

Breath echoed
against my empty heart.

Alone.
Alone.
Alone.

Death
  not an evil specter.
Nothing to fear
  offered reunion—
  Necha, Mama, Lázaro
maybe Tata and Iser.
Though I would not let myself think that.

Not yet.
Not yet.
Not yet.

Iser would live.
He would.
He would not let the Germans win.
I would not let the Germans win.
I had to tell Iser what happened to
  Mama, Lázaro, Necha.

Remember.
Remember.
Remember.

Knowing there were worse things than death
took away the fear.
Surviving was the best revenge.

Survive.
Survive.
Survive.

Watching

Our first day out of quarantine,
Zlatka helped carry back
A body.
I watched her
After *Appell*,
Face blank and pale.

I thought she might
Melt in despair
Into the softening ground.

She is going to die too,
I said.
Like Necha.
Bronia nodded.
Guta and Giza agreed.
But what can we do?

I approached Zlatka,
Like a frightened bird,
Every measured step a heartbeat.

Here,
I offered my ration of bread,
You must eat.

Zlatka's eyes,
Washed-out brown,
Looked through me.
Zlatka's lips,
Chapped and bleeding,
Remained closed.

I left the bread
In her lap
Whispered a prayer
That she'd eat it
Before someone
Stole it.

Folded Heart

I tucked thoughts of
Mama,
Papa,
Mushke,
In my heart.
Folded them away
For safekeeping.

But Leybl
Stayed constantly
In my thoughts,
Dreams,
Fears.
He would survive
I had to believe that.

Otherwise,
I was alone.
Completely.
With no one
To know my story,
To know who I had once been.
How much my family
Loved.
How much we laughed.

I told myself
Leybl was alive
Somewhere.
For all I knew
He was on the other side
Of the barbed-wire fence
That separated the men from the women.

I told myself
I was better off
Without Mama and Mushke to worry over.
I needed to fold up my heart
As small as possible
To survive.

Learning to Survive

Fearful
Of the Aryans who wore
Black or green triangles,
Vagrants, prostitutes, and criminals,
Believed in
The master race.

Fearful
Of anyone we didn't know
For even Jews would
Push in line,
Point an accusing finger,
Steal a crust of bread or bowl.

I did what I was told.
Kept my mouth shut
My eyes down.
Tried not to draw
Attention.

All around
Clumps of friends,
Of families,
Protected one another.

I stayed with the girls from Łomża
Bronia, Guta, Giza.

Zlatka was alone.

Friends

Watching Zlatka
Sink deeper into the mud of despair
A stab more painful
Than my tattoo.

I could have been her,
Lost Mushke here
Instead of in Białystok.
She could have been me,
Found friends
To keep her company.

We lost family too,
I told her.
Bronia, Guta, Giza by my side.

We are like you,
Jewish,
Polish,
Alone.
But not anymore.

We will stick close together
So no one will be alone
On a Kommando
At night in the Koje.

We will be each other's family.

I unfolded
   A corner of my heart.

74207

Just outside the barbed-wire fence,
A stand of birches.
I'd never seen trees the color of ghosts.

Bark streaked with black,
Lashes on the skin.
Blending with the
Winter sky,
Gray with billows of black smoke,
Snow-covered ground,
Trampled muddy footpaths.

My forearm,
   Thin as paper,
   Losing luster,
   Scarred with black.

The Orchestra

Music,
Soaring music,
Floated through the air
As we stood for *Appell*,
As *Kommandos*
Marched to work
And back again.
Music to keep us calm,
To help us forget
The chimneys,
Starvation,
Death.
Civility mingled with ash.

Not a full orchestra
But violins,
Mandolins,
A flute,
And double bass.
Women pulled from the transports
To play.

Eyes closed,
It sounded
Like the phonographs
Papa once played at home.

For a moment
I was transported
In time
And place
To safety
And love.

But it was just a moment.

Eyes opened
Back in the camp
I hated the women,
Prisoners,
Some with yellow stars,
Like me,
Wearing real clothes,
Not the coarse striped uniform,
But stolen clothes from off the transports,
Stored in warehouses we called *Kanada*—
A land of plenty, far away.

Their hair long enough to pull back,
Flesh on their bones,
Making beautiful music.
Entertaining the Nazis,
Making them smile
And laugh

As if they were human,
As if they knew beauty,
As if they had hearts,
As if they had souls.

A woman,
Eyes closed,
Sang an angel's song.
Her face
An expression
Of pure joy,
An emotion
I'd not seen for a long time.

But when she stopped singing,
Eyes opened,
Joy vanished.

I stared
And thought the woman
Caught my eye
But had to turn away.

Do you hate yourself
As much as I hate you?

The *Sonderkommando*

I thanked God
When we were assigned to a *Kommando*
Working inside the camp.
The *Aussenkommandos*,
Sent outside to do
Hard labor,
Were death sentences.

As I worked,
Laying cobblestones into the mud,
I watched.

The men of the *Sonderkommando*
Moved like ghosts
Among the living.
Carried corpses,
Ushered the selected.

Why do they do it?
I wondered.

The men of the *Sonderkommando*
Moved like ghosts
Among the dead.
Carried corpses,
Stoked the furnaces.

Doing dirty work for the Nazis,
I said.
They are monsters.

The men of the *Sonderkommando*
Moved like ghosts
Among themselves.
Spread the ashes,
And began again.

The Birds

Spring brought the rains
And the mud.

But no birds.

They avoided the belching black smoke,
Billowing stench,
Ash,
Impenetrable gray,
Incessant trains.

Later,
Much later,
People claimed,
  We did not know.
  I had no idea.
  I didn't do it.

How could they not have known,
When the birds did?

The Scent of Death

As constant as the ash,
A certain smell
Seeped under my skin.

I absorbed it,
Breathed it,
Knew it.

The perpetual possibility
Swelled inside my soul.

Transports

Trains arrived,
Dumping human cargo
Onto the *Judenrampe*.

Lost souls with bewildered faces
Moved along
Carrying suitcases,
Grasping children.
Pushed ahead by soldiers,
Barking dogs.
Dodging *Sonderkommandos*
Retrieving the dead.
Doing as they were told.

While the orchestra played.

An SS doctor,
A slightly built man
Standing as stiff
As the creases in his uniform pants
Pointed.
To the left.

                                                    To the right.

An SS officer called out,
Zwillinge!
Twins!
The doctor hurried over.

A third group,
   Neither left nor right.

What happens to them?
Zlatka asked.
Who knows,
I said.
Some things are worse than death,
Zlatka said.

New arrivals
Yelled through the barbed-wire fence,
Have you seen my husband, Shlomo?
I am looking for my wife, Rivka.
Have you heard of my cousin?
Is anyone from Łódź?

Zlatka watched.
Her shoulders straightening,
As if absorbing their anguish,
As if gaining strength.

I moved away.
Unable to relive,
Unable to witness
The loss.

The Men's Camp

Through the barbed wire
I could see men.

Gray-and-blue-clad shadows
Husbands,
Fathers,
Brothers,
Sons,
Lovers.

Too far away to speak,
I craned my neck,
Searching
For a familiar face.

Leybl?

My eyes followed a ghost.
Could it be?

The same tilt of his head.
The same height.
The same gait.

Leybl!

The figure moved away.

Leybl!

I ran along the fence,
My heart pounding.
Desperate for another look.

Too thin.
Too old.
Too gray.

Would I even recognize him?
Would he recognize me?

Leybl's ghost disappeared,
Faded into the gray.

I pressed down my folded heart
Unable to think of
Mama and Papa,
Mushke.

But Leybl will survive,
My words fell with the ash.

A hand around my shoulder.
Zlatka.

Come,
She whispered,
Leading me away from the wire,
Do not let them see you cry.

The Angel of Death

We began to see him
More often,
On the *Judenrampe*
Waiting for the transports
Watching.
Selecting.

Even
If another doctor
Was on duty.

Cold eyes
In a handsome face
Searched inside
Sensing something
Beneath the skin's surface.

The loud call of
Zwillinge!
Twins!
Caused commotion.

A flick of his riding crop.
To the left.

To the right.

A third group
That disappeared
Who knew where.

Whispers gathered.
Shivers of sweat
Tremors of terror
More than his cold-eyed stare,
Not knowing
What happened to the third group.

We did not know his name.
Yet we knew he was
The Angel of Death.

Nobodies

Zlatka and I
Passed by a group
Of Black Triangles,
Aryan girls
Who thought they were better.
Grabbing Zlatka's arm
I tried to walk faster.
I wanted
To run.
But Zlatka said,
Do not show your fear.
And walked by as if
On a stroll home from *shul*
On Friday night.

First came the word,
Juden!
Only a word,
Jews!
But on their lips,
A curse,
An insult,
A threat.
Then more words
Spat out
In a dialect

I was thankful
Not to understand.

I tried to walk faster.
I wanted
To run.
But Zlatka said,
They are nobodies.
And walked by as if
We were the only two people
On the earth.

Then came the stones,
Hard,
Sharp,
Painful
Against my arm.
Zlatka's head.
A trickle of blood
Down her temple.
She did not flinch.

I tried to walk faster.
I wanted
To run.
But Zlatka said,

They can only kill us.
And walked by as if
She were not afraid
Of death.

Back in the *Koje*
I cleaned Zlatka's wound
As best I could
With the hem of my striped uniform
And no water or soap.

Bronia, Guta, and Giza
Gathered round.
What happened?
Are you hurt?
Who did this?

I answered,
  Nobodies.
Zlatka smiled.

The Days of Awe

Took me by surprise.
Nine months had passed
In a moment,
An eternity.

In the autumn
As the leaves turn.
Ten days
Beginning with *Rosh Hashanah*,
The New Year,
Ending with *Yom Kippur*,
The Day of Atonement,
Filled with
Reflection,
Repentance,
Remembrance.

The *Unetaneh Tokef*,
A poem,
A prayer,
Meant to strike fear
Into those waiting for *Adonai*'s judgment.

As I chanted
I had no fear of God.

On Rosh Hashanah *it is written.*
On Yom Kippur *it is sealed.*
Who shall live.
Who shall die.
Who shall see ripe age and who shall not;
Who shall perish by fire and who by water;
Who by sword and who by beast;
Who by hunger and who by thirst;
Who by earthquake and who by plague;
Who by strangling and who by stoning.

Biblical means of death
Did not frighten me.

I had my own version:
It is written
And it is sealed
Every day.
Who shall live.
Who shall die.
Few of us will see ripe age and most shall not;
Who by beating and who by gas chamber;
Who by hunger and who by thirst;
Who by exhaustion and who by gunshot;
Who by exposure and who by dysentery;
Who by suicide and who by typhus.

In prayer,
God offers hope
In repentance, prayer and charity.

In reality,
The Germans did not.

Chapter 7

Zlatka

Kanada

In my dreams,
a land of plenty—
far away,
safe.

In reality,
warehouses—
stuffed with worldly possessions
from cardboard suitcases
  leather satchels
  canvas bags.

Mountains of
  clothing
  jewelry
  food
  blankets
  shoes
  treasured favorites

books
toy trains
and drawing sets.
Sorted by large-fisted Aryans
and shipped to Germany.

Kanada was *verboten*!

But goods could be had
for a price.
Pieces of a normal life
traded for bread.

How much for that pretty purple blouse?
   I asked.
Too much for a dirty Jew,
   answered a broad-faced Aryan girl.
How much for that pretty purple blouse?
   I asked,
Again.

Why do you want it?
   Bronia asked.
Why take the risk?
   Guta wondered.
Why pay the price?
   Giza said.

To feel pretty again,
  I answered.

I paid the price,
  a day's ration of bread.
And didn't mind
  when my stomach growled
  all night.

Fania passed me her bread.
I'm not really hungry,
  she said with a wink.

When I dressed in the morning
  a whisper of silk
  lay hidden
  between my skin
  and the coarseness of my
  striped uniform.

Another Selection

We stood together
  Fania and I
behind us,
  Bronia, Guta, and Giza
waiting.
Clutching
each other's hands.

I smoothed down my dress
examined fingernails
  as if waiting for approval
  from Mama before going
  to *shul*.

Anticipation
dripped down my spine
  a trickle of sweat on a hot day.

Watching the girls before us
some moved to the left

                                        some to the right.

No rhyme
  or reason.

Huddled against Fania
waiting.

Clutching
each other's hands.

How do I look?
Am I too thin?
  Fania asked.

I saw myself
reflected in Fania
  deprivation and decay
carved on her face
wafting off her skin.

You look beautiful,
  I assured her.

I pinched my cheeks
for color
  as I'd once done while
  waiting for a date.

But this was not
a handsome boy
meeting me with a smile.

How do I look?
Am I too pale?
  I asked Fania.

Fania tilted her head
  examining
  smiling.

You look beautiful,
  Fania assured me.

Still
fear lashed
my bony spine
  like a riding crop.

One by one
we stood
before him.
SS captain.
German doctor.
  The Angel of Death
We called him.

Me first,
  chin up
  eyes straight ahead
  fists clenched.
His cold-eyed stare
seeping through me.
Then Fania,
  chin tucked

eyes cast down
hands clasped before her.

Turned.
Poked
and prodded.

Then Bronia
Guta
Giza.

Hugs
Smiles
Relief.
Exhilarating
Exhausting.

Existing

Worn as thin as a striped uniform,
   memory frayed
   existence disintegrated
   time unraveled.

Death slept beside me
   every night.
Sat beside me
   every day.

Only the wheezing of
   breath in, then out,
   the beat of my heart
   reminded me I was still alive.

I raised my head
   looked past the gray
   past the gruesomeness
   and looked to the horizon.

At Breakfast

Giza cried,
Where's my bowl?
It was just here!
I turned my back for a moment!

Others moved away,
   shoulders curled
   protecting
   their own
   bowls.

How am I going to eat?

We crowded around,
   hands outstretched
   offering
   our own
   bowls.

Out of Step

Standing in *Appell*
  after everyone was counted
we split into our *Kommandos*.
Lining up
  perfect formation
to march off to work.

Fania and I
stood next to each other.
The overseer
  burly
  German guard
shouted
the order to march.
We all stepped forward
left
  right
left
  right.

Except Fania
who stepped forward
  right
left
  right
left.

The overseer yanked Fania
   out of line.
The riding crop lashed.
Once
Twice
   across her back.
The *Kapo*
   joined in.
A billy club beat.
Once
Twice
   in her gut.

The overseer shoved Fania
   back in line
and watched her hobble forward
left
   right
left
   right.

I reached out
   squeezed Fania's hand.
Do not let them
see you cry,
   I whispered.
Do not let them
change who you are.

Fania swallowed her tears
and marched on
left
  right
left
  right.

Strength

At midday
   I shared my bread with Fania.
To keep you strong,
   I told her when she protested.

Fania chewed,
   not minding the staleness
      mold
      weevils.

I try,
   Fania said,
to do as I am told.
I try
to be good
to not draw attention
to get by.
I must survive
for Leybl.
He will need me.
But how can I?
When being good is not
good enough?

I looked away
   toward the horizon.
When I spoke,

my voice a trace
    a whisper
    a secret.

Papa told me
never to forget
that we all carry
a spark of God.
  No matter what they do
they cannot take
the tiny piece of
God
away.

They cannot take my thoughts.
I remember
  who I am
  who I was
  my family
  my life.

Survival is a balance
between being good
  and bad
between being strong
  and weak.
You cannot be

too much of
anything
   or they will notice
they will take you,

I whispered to Fania,
but was speaking to
myself.

I will survive.
I will not give the Germans
the satisfaction
of dying.

At Dinner

Fania appeared
  still limping
with an extra bowl.

She handed it to
Giza
without a word.

I didn't ask
  none of us
asked
where she got it.

Budding Love

Bronia and Giza worked to lay stones in the roadway
  over the endless mud.
Guta, Fania, and I worked dredging filth
  from the ditches
  bordering the crematorium.

We took turns keeping watch
  and resting
  when no one was looking.

Other girls flirted
through the barbed wire
surrounding Crematorium II
with the men
in the *Sonderkommando*.
One girl
  her eyes shadowed
  darker than the night
pressed her lips
between the barbed wire for a kiss.

How can you talk to them?
  Guta asked.
They are monsters,
  Fania said.
Doing dirty work for the Germans,
  I said.

Defense of the *Sonderkommando*

The girl replied,
They are no more monster
than you.

My brother
was selected
for the Sonderkommando
when we first arrived.
I used to meet him
  here at the fence
so he could unburden
his soul.

Yes,
he helped the Germans.
He led people,
  innocent people
  children,
to their deaths.

He whispered
assurances to them.
Calmed them
so their last moments
were not filled with terror.

He spread their ashes
  with respect
  due to humans.
He said Kaddish *for them*
  mourned them.

His first assignment
  fresh off the transport
was to gas
the Sonderkommando
he replaced.

His last assignment
  just three months later
was to walk
  with dignity
into the gas chamber
so the new Sonderkommando
could replace him.

The Sonderkommando
are not monsters.

Terrible Irony

Wrought in iron
hanging over the gate.

Hanging over my head
Every
single
day.

ARBEIT MACHT FREI
Work will set you free.

The biggest lie
  the biggest truth.

Belgian Beauty

We all knew
Mala Zimetbaum.
She'd been in the camp
longer than most.

She survived because
she was beautiful
  brilliant
  bold.

So beautiful
  the Germans
  did not cut her long blond hair
  did not make her dress
      in the coarse uniform.

So bright
  the Germans
  made her a *Läuferin*
      a messenger
      with privileges and responsibilities
      running all over the camp
      translating French, Dutch, Italian, and Polish.

So bold
   she used her beauty and brilliance
   to help
   whenever she could.
Moving through the camp
   on errands of mercy.

The Germans noticed
   her pretty smile
   sashaying hips
   lighthearted laugh.
They did not notice
   the photographs
         she sneaked out of files,
   the sweaters
         she stole from *Kanada*,
   the prisoners
         whose work details she switched,
   the medicine
         she swiped from the prisoners' hospital.

We all loved
Mala Zimetbaum.

Chapter 8

Fania

Rumors

I heard rumors
Of a new *Kommando*.
A factory
That would make buttons,
Bowls,
Bicycles.

If we joined,
We would get
More food,
More heat.
We would not
Work outdoors,
Go through Selections.

Should we volunteer?
  Zlatka asked.
What if it's a lie?
  Guta asked.

Bronia answered,
 Then we die.
What if it's the truth?
 Giza asked.
Then we live,
 Bronia answered.

We were told,
 We need metallurgists.
We nodded,
 Agreed,
 Yes, we are metallurgists.

What's a metallurgist?
 Guta asked.
Shhh, I don't know,
 I answered,
But if that is what I have to be
 That is what I will be.
What if they find out?
 Giza asked.
Shhh, I don't know,
 I said.

One more Selection.
One more parade of naked women

Before a doctor.
Not the Angel of Death.

To the left.

                                    To the right.

                                        We all
                            Joined the new *Kommando*.

Privileges

The new *Kommando* also brought privileges.
The new *Block*
Had a furnace.
More food
To keep up our strength.
And new clothes.

We had to look nice,
As if we were not starving
Or in fear for our lives.
At the factory,
We would work
With people from outside the camp.

We got new
Slips,
Panties,
Stockings,
Dresses,
Sweaters
From *Kanada*.
Better than what we had before
But not as nice as what was
Shipped to Germany
Or traded for a profit.

Not as pretty as the purple blouse
Zlatka still wore
Hidden under her uniform.

Clean Clogs

The overseer marched before us
Riding crop tight in her hand.
The *Kapos* scampered behind,
Faithful dogs.

They inspected and counted
Hundreds of women
Standing in perfect
Blocks of five.

Other *Kommandos* marched off.
But we stood still.
The factory wasn't ready.
Instead of working
We stood for hours in *Appell*.

In the mud that still oozed
Between the paving stones
In the chill autumn air.
For hours
Each day.
Day after day.

My mind wandered
I unfolded the memories in my heart
Platters of food,

Hot baths,
Clean sheets,
Boys who smiled,
Studying with Leybl,
But crumpled it back up
When memories became too painful.

Some girls fell ill.
Fainted.
Exhausted.
Starving.
They were taken to the prisoners' hospital,
Never to be seen again.

When the whistles finally announced
The end of *Appell*
We returned to the *Block*
Only to be beaten by the *blockova*.
Lashed with a whip,
Hair pulled,
Because our wooden clogs were dirty.

You are part of the Union Kommando,
  She screamed.
Do not bring shame!

Some cleaned their shoes in puddles.
I gathered what spittle I had

And spat upon them.
Wiping my shoes clean
With dirty hands.

Marching

Finally, after weeks of waiting,
One morning after *Appell*
We marched off
As the orchestra played.

Left,
  Right.
Left,
  Right.

Eyes front.
Lines straight.

Left,
  Right.
Left,
  Right.

Past the guards and their dogs.
Past the SS officers.

Left,
  Right.
Left,
  Right.

Through the gates.
Far from the strains of the orchestra.

Left,
   Right.
Left,
   Right.

Out of the shadow of the chimneys.
Beyond the stench of the smoke.

Left,
   Right.
Left,
   Right.

Feet ached.
Feet swelled.

Left,
   Right.
Left,
   Right.

Keeping in step.
Doing what I was told.

But looking toward the horizon,
  Like Zlatka,
To see what it was she saw.

Weichsel Union Metallwerke

Enormous.
Red brick.
Windowless,
  But for skylights.
Surrounded,
Like everything else,
By a tall barbed-wire fence.

Inside,
Air thickened by
Thrumming machines,
No windows,
Hundreds of workers.

Stifling noises
Pulsed off the walls,
Pushed against my body,
Pressed me until I barely existed at all.

Yellow dust
Lingered in the air
Coated every surface.

Sweat-soaked men
In blue-gray uniforms
Worked the *Pressen*,

Monstrous machines,
With heavy pistons
That rose and lowered
Every three minutes
Spitting out yellow dust.

The *Weichsell Union Metallwerke*
Did not make buttons,
Bowls,
Or bicycles.

We made armaments.

Weapons.
Bullets.
Shells.
Grenades.

I'd volunteered
Thinking I'd be safe.
Now I worked
Making weapons
To fight those who
Tried to free us.

We are no better than the
Sonderkommandos.

We are monsters,
   I said,
Doing dirty work for the Germans.

No! Zlatka was firm.
We are surviving.

Control Section

The work was easy.
Child's play.
Empty shells
From the *Pressen*,
Warm and coated in yellow dust,
Needed to be measured.
Precise.
Monotonous.
Continual.
Mindless.

My mind numbed
From boredom.
My body ached
From repetition.

There were consequences
For mistakes.
Sabotage!
Would bring a beating.
If you were lucky.

The work was easy.
Child's play.
Empty shells
From the *Pressen*,
Warm and coated in yellow dust,

Needed to be measured.
Precise.
Monotonous.
Continual.
Mindless.

My body moved
Like a marionette.
The edges of my heart
  Unfolded.

There were consequences
For thinking.

Always Watched

Glass walls separated departments:
Conveyor Belt,
Control Section,
Gunpowder,
Machine Shop.

Every department watched by:
SS guards,
Kapos,
Meisters,
Overseers.

The day scheduled:
Break in the morning
To use the toilet,
Break at noon
To eat lunch,
Break in the afternoon
To use the toilet.

The only place
We were not watched
Was the lavatory
Where women lingered
To gossip
Make exchanges,

Bread for cigarettes,
Gather information.

Sometimes it was too crowded
To use the toilet.

I kept my head down
Focused on my work.
Tried not to think
Of the soldiers
Who would be killed
With the bullets
I was making.

Comrades

Twenty-one girls
Sat at one long table.

Eighteen of us were Polish.

Two were French.

One was German.

All were Jews.

The French Girls

For most of us,
Yiddish
Was our mother tongue,
The blend of Hebrew and German,
Rolled in our mouths,
Like sweets on *Rosh Hashanah*.

I could understand
Most of the Germans.
Enough to do as I was told.
But some spoke dialects
Too rough upon
My ears.

I also spoke Polish
And a little Russian,
Since Mama and Papa
Had spoken it
In the house
When I was young.

Zlatka also spoke
Yiddish,
Polish,
And Russian,
Much better than I,
And understood German.

We could talk
With almost everyone
In the camp.

Except the French girls
  Eva
  Hélène
Only spoke French.

Still,
A smile,
A frown,
Tears,
And laughter
Were understood in any language.

Meister Eberhart Smiled

I sat at our table,
Precisely measuring
Shells.
Tossing away
Those that
Did not
Conform.
Occasionally,
  When I was sure
  No one was looking,
Allowing one
To slip by.

The *Meister*
Walked by.
Stopped.
Watched.

Foolishly,
I looked up.
He caught my eye.
Smiled.
Even more foolishly,
I returned his smile.
A reflex
From another world,
Where smiles

Were returned,
Not regretted,
Or suspicious.
The *Meister*
Then walked on.

Why did he smile at me?
  I whispered.
Maybe he admires your
Beautiful hair?
  Zlatka said.
We all laughed,
Even the French girls.

Maybe he was just
Being kind?
  Bronia said.
Which made us all laugh
Louder.

At Night

After we marched
Back to the camp.
After we stood in *Appell*.
After the orchestra
Stopped playing.
After we chewed
A hard ration of bread.
After prayers
Floated toward the rafters.

Sleep came
As hard
Though not as permanent
As death.

For in the morning,
It all began again.
Doing as we were told.

Mornings

The day began
Before the sun was up.
Alle raus!
Everybody out!
Mach schnell!
Make it quick!

I stumbled
From our bunk.
Hastily gathered my belongings
Bowl,
Spoon,
Scrap of soap,
Comb,
Zlatka slipped her pretty purple blouse
Beneath her uniform.

A stampede for the *Waschraum*.
Bodies pushed and shoved.

Halt! ordered the *blockova*,
Particularly nasty.
No more in the Waschraum.

But we need to wash,
    A stupid girl said.

The *blockova*'s fists were
Fierce and frightening
Heavy and hateful.

Zlatka,
Bronia,
Guta,
Giza,
And I
Returned to the *Block*.

Took turns
Squatting over the bucket.

Playing Cards

Giza organized a deck of cards
From *Kanada*.
Half a day's ration of bread.
A small price to pay
For evening entertainment.

We played rummy.
Four at a time.
Taking turns
While one watched
For the *blockova*.

Lying on our bunk.
Laughing.
Pretending we were somewhere else.

A Blatant Lie

I woke one morning
My back prickled
With sweat
Despite the frost from my mouth
When I breathed.

Bronia, Guta, and Giza
Climbed from the *Koje*.
I followed
But Zlatka remained,
Her pale cheeks
Flushed red,
Her smooth forehead
Beaded with sweat.

Unsteady on her feet—
I helped Zlatka stand in line
For her morning ration.
I said,
  You'll feel better
  Once you eat.
She smiled and said,
  Yes, wouldn't we all.

The *blockova* stared hard
At Zlatka.

Is she sick?
  She asked.
No, no, no,
  I said.
Sickness would send Zlatka
To *Block* 25
Like her sister
Necha.

No, no, no,
  I said,
  Convincing myself
  More than the *blockova.*
It's just …
She has …
It's her time of month.

It was absurd.
None of us had bled
  In months
  In a year.
But it was all
That came to mind.
I looked the *blockova*
Right in the eye
  Without flinching
And lied.

It was absurd.
So absurd
She believed me.
Who would tell such a blatant lie?

I gave Zlatka my morning ration.
Left her with Bronia, Guta, and Giza.
Ran to find Mala Zimetbaum.
If Mala could get aspirin,
Even just a few,
Zlatka's fever would pass.

Marching to the factory
Sweat dripped down my back
Despite the cold.
My heart climbed
With every step
Up my throat.
If Zlatka stumbled,
Fell behind,
Collapsed
They would take her away.

We marched
Around her
Bronia,
Guta,
Giza,

And I
Trying to keep her hidden
Trying to keep her moving.

Zlatka marched,
Her face burning
With fever
As if her spine were made
Of steel.

At work
At the table
All the girls
Worked harder
To do Zlatka's
Portion.
She rested
When no one was looking.
Looked busy
When the *Kapo*
Came by.

That night
In the *Block*
A packet
From Mala.

Four small aspirin.

A gift.
A miracle.
A life.

In two days
Zlatka's fever broke.

Zlatka never did.

The Bravery of Kindness

You lied,
   Zlatka whispered,
      Her forehead free from
      Beads of sweat
      Her cheeks no longer
      Burning.
I didn't think
A good girl
Like you
Could lie.

I laughed.
   I didn't think I could either.
   But what else
   Could I do?

Some people,
   She said,
Would have done nothing.
Would have let them
Take me.
Would have thought
Only of themselves.

   Arms wide,
I said,
   I didn't do
      Anything special.

I didn't ignore
  Tormenting Black Triangles.
I didn't march
  Three kilometers with a raging fever.
I didn't dare to wear
  A pretty purple blouse.

Zlatka smiled.
No, instead,
  She said,
You befriended me
  When I was lost.
You stole a bowl for Giza
  When hers was missing.
You shared your ration with me
  When you were hungry.

Your kindness, Fania,
Makes me brave.

I could not speak.
My cheeks burned
But not with fever.

Your bravery, Zlatka,
Makes me kind.

Chapter 9

Zlatka

Power Outages

At least once a week
  the lights went out.
The *Pressen* stopped.
The machinery stilled.
The yellow dust settled
  slowly on the floor.

I stretched my arms
  up to heaven
enjoying the rest from work
  the rest from being watched.

The *Meisters*
  Overseers
  Guards
  Kapos
stood apart.
Meisters yelling
  at the overseers.

Overseers yelling
  at the guards.
Guards yelling
  at the *Kapos*.

The *Kapo* came
  to our table.
Finish the work you have!
  she yelled.

I continued
measuring
shells
  precisely.
Tossing away
those that
did not
  conform.

When there were no more
shells to measure
we talked
  in hushed whispers
so the *Kapo*
would not hear.

We told each other
our stories.
I am from Prużany.
I am from Białystok.
A village in the north.
From Munich.
De Paris.
I was the eldest of four.
I was the middle of seven.
I was in school.
Me too.
I worked in a store.
I had a boyfriend.
Me too.
I wonder where he is now.
Sometimes at night
        I dream of him.
Sometimes at night
        I dream of brisket.
Of kasha.
Of latkes.
Of pierogi.

My Hands

should have been
  soft
  clean
  dainty,
should have been
  caressed
  by a boy my age.

Instead,
my hands worked
  twelve hours a day.
Measured and checked,
  shell after shell,
  after shell.
Precise.
Exact.

My skin
  as thin as a whisper
  knuckles protruding,
  ragged dirty nails.
Hands like a *bubbe*, not nineteen.

I watched my hands,
  imagined
holding colored pencils

imagined
drawing the horizon
in vivid color.

Girl Talk

Will my hair grow back?
Will my stomach ever be full?
Will I celebrate another birthday?
Will I ever light Shabbos *candles again?*

Will I ever see Warsaw again?
Will I wear real shoes?
Will I eat apples and honey on Rosh Hashanah*?*
Will I have a home?

Will I fall in love?
Will I stand under the wedding chuppah*?*
Will I have children?
Will I grow old?

Will I wake up tomorrow?
Will I survive?

Living Corpses

The overseer and the *Kapos*
walked through the factory
  stopping at every table.

What are they looking for?
  someone asked.
Muselmanns,
  someone answered.

Muselmanns
  thin as skeletons
  joints protruding
  dead though they still lived.

  Too weak to move
        to work
        to care.

  Ordered to *Block* 25.
  Gone with no complaints.

The overseer and the *Kapos*
walked through the factory
  stopping at every table.
Staring.
Their eyes like X-rays
looking through striped uniforms.

I kept working.
Pretended they were not there.
Busy with work.
Thankful their eyes
    could not really see through striped uniforms.

Kontrolle!

Fear rippled through the air.
Work stopped.
Kapos descended.
Searches conducted.

They looked for smugglers
    stealing gunpowder.
But confiscated everything
    comb
    toothbrush
    deck of playing cards
Everything from *Kanada*.
Even
    a pretty purple blouse.

What is this?
    The *Kapo* asked.
My blouse,
    I answered.
The *Kapo*'s face softened
    into something wistful
    as if remembering
    what it was like
    to wear
    something soft.
She looked around.

Don't let me see it again,
  she said, walking away.

The next morning, I put on my
  pretty purple blouse.

Again.

Lockdown

Large transports
  bigger than ever
arrived.
The entire camp
  except for the orchestra
went into *Blocksperre*.
Confined to our *Blocks*.
Windows shuttered closed.
Hours passed.

Through the battered walls
we heard music
  soaring music.

I imagined
hundreds off the trains.
  Jews.
  Roma.
  Families.
  Old.
  Young.

Music played
to soothe us all.

Locked inside
the girls and I trembled
  a mix of fear
  and anger
      knowing.
Until the Selection was done.

And the chimneys belched more smoke.

Escape!

Mala!
  Our Belgian beauty
With her boyfriend
  Edek Galinski!

Escape
was unimaginable.

We all cheered.

The Germans fumed.

Blocksperre for hours
  as the Germans searched.

Locked in our *Blocks*
  the girls and I prayed
        hoped
        wished
  for Mala's success.

We huddled together.
Voices hushed but euphoric.
If anyone can escape,
  Bronia said,
it is Mala.

She can blend in,
    Guta said.
And she speaks so many languages,
    Giza said.
She is not a Muselmann, *skin and bones,*
    Fania said,
    hugging her own skinny frame.
She still has her hair.
    I ran my hand over my shorn scalp.

A Miracle

Mrs. Grosman
slept in the bunk below
  Fania
  Bronia
  Guta
  Giza
  and me.
She wrote a letter
to her husband.

A miracle.

It didn't matter
  when she wrote it
  how she got the paper
  how she got the pencil.
All that mattered
  was that she'd written it.

A miracle.

If she'd written it
  a year ago
  and kept it hidden.

If she'd written it
   last week
   and kept it hidden.
Who cared?

A miracle.

As far as she knew
   he was free
   he was alive.

A miracle.

Every night
Mrs. Grosman read her letter
   like a prayer.
A love letter
lulled me to sleep.
   A lullaby.

Then—
   the *blockova*
found it
confiscated it

handed it over
to the SS *Kommandant* of the female camp.

On a bright spring morning
while we stood
in *Appell*
Mrs. Grosman
was hanged.

A lesson not to believe in miracles.

Coping

Upwind from the chimneys
blue sky hung like a promise
in the air.

Bronia, Guta, Giza,
Fania, and I
held hands in the unexpected
sunshine.

It was easy to remember
the way life used to be—
the way life should be—
the way life could be
Again.

I lifted my hand to the sky
toward the horizon.
Spring fluttered
warm and gentle
through my fingers
radiating to the others
a wave of hope
a current of belief
that this would not go on
forever.

Three other girls
holding hands
walked past us
toward the
shadow of the chimneys.

On the beautiful blue-sky day
when hope hung like
cotton-ball clouds
one girl lifted her hand to the fence
toward the signs that warned
ACHTUNG! LEBENSGEFAHR!

Death rippled
through her fingers
radiated to the others.
A wave.
A current.
The end.

Why Me?

I asked
every night
when I lay down to sleep.

Why do I continue
  when so many have given up?

I asked
every morning
when I opened my eyes.

Why am I alive
  when the rest of my family is gone?

I drew pictures
in my mind
  a house filled with love
     books
     train sets
     pads of paper and colored pencils,
     a strand of paper dolls, cut precisely
  my family together
    for Shabbos.

I remembered Tata's voice
  his lips upon my forehead.
No matter what comes,

always remember who you are.
No one can take that from you.

One more glance
   out the tiny sealed window
at the horizon,
then I climbed down the *Koje*
ready to start the day.

———

Captured

First we heard the whispers—
  Mala and Edek have been caught.
  Edek was arrested in a nearby town.
  Mala turned herself in
      to be with him.

Then the rumors—
  Mala and Edek are in prison Block *11*
      as suspected saboteurs.
  Mala and Edek are being tortured.
  Mala and Edek are dead.

What is happening?
  we all wondered.
Was Mala caught?
  we all whispered.

All we knew for certain,
  whatever was happening
it was not good.

Small Gestures

Meister Eberhart
smiled a lot
    at everyone
as he watched
from his glass-walled office.

Daily
he walked
through the factory,
rolled a cigarette,
lit it
    while he watched
    the men work the *Pressen*.
He took a drag,
set it down,
and walked off
only to roll another,
light it,
set it down,
and walk off again.
He looked away
    when the men picked up
    the cigarettes.

One day
I watched him
give a package

to a girl
two tables over.

I heard
  later
the package
had a sausage
hidden in it.

Chapter 10

Fania

More Rumors

Floated in the wind
Landed on my eager ears.
Stories of
  A massive invasion.
Allied troops
  British,
  American
Drawing nearer.
Day
By
Day.

News

Spread from lips to ears
  The way lice and fleas
Jumped from body to head.

News,
  Any news,
Made me itch
With excitement.

Word spread
  Through an invisible line of resistance
From the Polish underground
To the camp
That the Red Army
Neared Warsaw.

Warsaw!
So close!

I've been to Warsaw,
  Zlatka said.
I won a prize as a schoolgirl.
I took a train by myself.
I'd never seen such a
  Magnificent city.

Bronia said,
   If the Russians
   Take Warsaw,
   Surely it will be just a matter of time
   Before they get here.
   The end
   Is near!

But,
   I asked,
What does the end
Mean for us?
Will the Germans
Stoke the fires
In the chimneys
And finish us all?

The end was near.

Public Punishment

On September 15, 1944,
During *Appell*
While we all
Stood in perfect lines,
And all the men,
   On the other side of the barbed wire,
Stood in perfect lines
Mala and Edek
Were dragged
To scaffolds.
Edek in the men's camp.
Mala in the women's.

I could not to see
Edek,
But I heard him cry out,
   Long live Poland!
The last word strangled in his throat.

Mala,
   Still beautiful, brilliant, and bold
   Though bloodied
Cut her wrists
With a dull razor
Before the hangman could do his job.

The Germans
Tried to save her
Binding her wounds
So she would die on their terms
   Not on her own.

Mourning

For seven days we sat *shiva*
   Grieving.

Silence
   Saturated
   With sorrow
Hung over the camp.

We did not play cards,
Talk,
Dream,
Or even sleep.

Minyans formed
To say *Kaddish*,
   Even though we were girls.

We all said
The *Shema*.

Even though I was sure
God was not listening.

Another New Year

Time did not exist,
Just existing.
Days did not matter,
Only surviving to the next.
Yet someone knew
It was the first day of *Tishri*.
The day God
Created Adam and Eve.
The first day
Of the Jewish year.
Rosh Hashanah.
L'shana tova.
Happy New Year.
Again.
My second
In hell.

In huddled groups
We proclaimed,
   Silently,
God as the one and only.
We repented
Our sins
And arrogance.
Asked forgiveness.

Granted forgiveness,
   Though not to everyone,
And prayed for a sweet New Year.

God decided
If our names would be written
In the Book of Life,
   Who shall live
   And who shall die.

But God had not been the one
Making those decisions
For many years.

Meister Eberhart's Good Girl

Autumn storms
Turned the gray sky
Grayer.
No sun
Sifted through
The skylights
To mingle with
The yellow dust.

Rain pelted down,
Tears shed by God
And all His angels.

We kept working
Faster,
Harder,
Longer.
Turning out
More.

 Weapons.
Bullets.
Shells.
Grenades.

The end of my shift,
Ready to start

The long march
Back,
Meister Eberhart
Motioned me over,
   A wave of his hand,
   A thin smile on his face.

I hesitated,
Looked between
My friends
   Zlatka,
   Bronia,
   Guta,
   Giza,
And the German *Meister*.

There were stories.
We all knew
Some poor girl
   Not given any choice,
   Unable to say No.
But surely not *Meister* Eberhart.
He had been kind.
Abandoned cigarettes.
Gave smiles and sausages.

He motioned again.

Go,
    Said the overseer,
    Her riding crop at my back,
    A smirk on her face,
As if I deserved
Whatever *Meister* Eberhart
Wanted me for.

I sucked in
Lungs full
Of the heavy, damp gray air.
Put my faith in *Adonai.*
Tried to remember
What Zlatka had said—
    They cannot take my thoughts.
Stepped forward.

Alone
With *Meister* Eberhart.
He grasped my hands.
His palms,
    Cold and sweaty,
Held me tight.
He fumbled inside
His suit coat.

Eyes squeezed shut,
Trying to shut out

Whatever
Was coming.

You are a good girl,
    He said,
    His voice raspy in my ear.

Meister Eberhart
Pressed something hard into my hands
A package wrapped in cloth,
    An old handkerchief.
He said,
    I'm sorry I can't do more.
He was gone.

Later,
In the *Koje,*
    In darkness,
    And silence,
Zlatka,
Bronia,
Guta,
Giza,
And I
Had a feast,
    A few bites,
Of cheese
    Smooth,

Creamy,
Delicious.

I sent a prayer
Asking for *Meister* Eberhart's forgiveness
Into the rafters.

Fears for the *Sonderkommando*

The girl met her lover
By Crematorium IV.

He passed her parcels
Of food and clothing.

She held his hand.
He whispered in her ear.

Tears streaked her face.
A frown furrowed his brow.

At night in the *Block*
She sobbed into her hands.

The transports are slowing down,
　She confided to me.

That's good,
　I answered.

The girl raised her tearstained cheeks.
Yes, but
What will become of the Sonderkommando?

I could not bring
Myself to answer.
I knew
The *Sonderkommando*
  Would be next
  To fuel the chimneys.

Something

Sizzled
In the air.
Crackled
Like electricity
Through
The camp fences.

Are the rumors true?

Something
Slithered
In the guards.
Strengthening
Their fists
As hard
As rocks.

Are the Russians getting closer?

Something
Slowed
The dreaded
Trains.
Lessened
The number sent
To the left

                         To the right.

Will I be here when they get here?

What was the point
Of suffering for so long
Only to die when
The end was near?

October 7, 1944

On a bright autumn day
We worked
Like it was any other day.

But soon
We inhaled
The tension
Of the guards,
  The *Kapos*,
  The overseers,
  The *Meisters*
Like we inhaled
The yellow dust
That sifted in the air.

Whispers
Across worktables,
In the lunch line,
In the lavatory,
What is happening?
I don't know.
What's going on?
I don't know.

Through the day
My eyes
Stayed on my work

So not to draw attention,
   Anger,
   A beating,
   Or worse.

Through the day
My ears
Stayed wide open
To gather information.

Through the day
My lungs
Filled with
Yellow dust,
   Fear,
   Hope.

Revolt!

I heard bits of the story
Standing at *Appell*,
Waiting in line,
  At the *Waschraum*,
  For evening ration.
Whispered among the *blockovas*,
  Kapos,
  Guards.

The *Sonderkommando*
Revolted!

Such bravery.
What courage.

Many tried to escape.
Running
Toward the woods.
Most were gunned down
Before
They got there.

The entire squad
Of the *Sonderkommando*
From Crematorium IV
Was shot.

But not before
Killing
Three SS corporals
And wounding many others.

Not before
Blowing up
Crematorium IV.
Destroying
  Walls,
  Furnace,
  Chimneys,
  Evil.

The Sonderkommando
  Are not monsters,
Zlatka said.

Better to die fighting
  Than live doing just what you are told,
I said.

A New *Block*

With the bite
Of coming winter
We,
  The entire
  Union Kommando,
Moved into a new *Block*
In Auschwitz.

Closer to the factory.
New,
Clean,
Big
With two-tiered bunks,
    Real mattresses,
    Blankets for everyone,
    A lavatory
      With showers,
      And hot water.

Why?
Why now?
Who cares.
Nothing the Germans do
  Makes sense,
  Why should this?
Just enjoy!

Investigations

Determined to discover
How the *Sonderkommando*
Got gunpowder,
The Germans
Crawled over
The *Weichsel Union Metallwerke.*

Watching.
Questioning.
Inspecting.
Even closer than before.

Finally,
Two girls
  I did not know,
Who worked in the gunpowder room,
  Ala Gertner,
  Estusia Wajcblum,
And a third girl
Who worked in a clothing *Kommando*,
  Roza Robota,
Were taken to *Block* 11.

Air Raids

Bombs fell
From heaven,
   Answers to my prayers.

The walls,
   Roof,
   Foundations,
Of the Union factory
Shook
With the might
Of *Adonai*.

I heard
The far-off
Rumble of airplanes,
   Welcomed like the
   Sound of thunder
   On a hot summer's day.

I smelled
Burning in the
Distance.
Imagined
Warming my hands
By the flames of their destruction.

The Germans,
  Meisters,
  Overseers,
  Guards,
Took cover
Outside the factory
Leaving us in
God's hands.

I was not afraid.

We crouched
Under our table.
Delighted.
Laughing.
Cheering.
Listening.

Zlatka smiled,
Fingers in her ears,
And yelled,
  That is the most beautiful sound in all the world!

No matter how it ended,
  The end was near.

Return from *Block* 11

A few weeks later,
Ala Gertner,
Roza Robota,
Estusia Wajcblum
Returned.

I saw them
Across the *Block.*
Bruised.
Broken.
Barely recognizable.

Only for a few days.
Then, they
And Regina Safirztajn,
    Supervisor of the gunpowder room,
Were taken away
Again.

Changes

Transports stopped
Arriving.

The chimneys stopped
Belching.

What was left of the *Sonderkommando*
Dismantled
Crematorium III
Brick
By brick
By brick.

What else
Will the Nazis destroy
To cover up
Their crimes?

Expectations

Life in Auschwitz
Had never been
Predictable.

Life in Auschwitz
Had no
Understandable rules.

I expected
Chaos,
Fear,
Beatings.

I expected
To die before I turned twenty.

But the growing certainty
That the Germans were losing,
That the Soviets were close,
   The flicker of hope
   That I might survive,
Was more frightening
   Than death.

Approaching Birthday

I did not know the date
Or even the month.
But I knew from the changing seasons,
   Autumn chilling into winter,
My birthday
Was fast approaching.

Birthdays at home
Had been full of love,
Family,
Presents,
And cake.

Birthdays belonged
In the past.
Folded tight,
Tucked away,
With memories
   Mama,
   Papa,
   Mushke,
   Leybl.

Birthdays did not belong
In Auschwitz
Where I did not know

If I would live another day
Let alone
Until my birthday.

Chapter 11

Zlatka

My Idea

I had lost my family.
Fania was like my sister
  now—
Sisters
  we each
   had lost.

I didn't know when
  I got the idea
  or how
but I knew I
  had to do something.
Something greater than
  gazing at the horizon
   wearing a pretty purple blouse.

Fania's birthday
  was coming.
She'd been sixteen

when the Germans came,
Just eighteen
when she was captured in Augustów.
Now Fania was turning twenty.

Who knew
   if we would live another day
   let alone
       to celebrate another birthday.

Everything in life passes by like a wave

over a rushing river

Only true love stays faithful forever

Love

To sweet Fani

Written by Zlatka

Auschwitz

12/XII/1944

I wish you luck, happiness, freedom,

written into your own [...]

Bronia

In Whispers

at night.
In quiet
  conversations.
I told the others.

Without Fania
  suspecting.
Without the *Kapo*
  knowing.
Without the guards
  seeing.

All of them
agreed.

Even the French girls
  who didn't understand
  a word I spoke.

My hearty wishes and achievements
Sent by Guta and Tonia
11/XII

Faniezka!
Don't cry when you are suffering,
don't let down your hand
The one that is strong will win, the
one who is down will perish!
Tonia and Gusia

Getting Supplies

Kanada
    had supplies.
But at a cost.

Paper
was expensive.
A pencil—
    a single pencil—
was a day's ration of bread.
Scissors were unattainable.
Too dangerous to buy.

The costs were high
    to own the forbidden.
Just ask Mrs. Grosman.

All the girls
chipped in
    shared bread rations
    negotiated deals
    hid the contraband

from the *Kapos*
from Fania.

My beautiful Fania
A lot of luck and freedom
Wishes
Giza

For pleasant memories
Rachela

Stealing

Bronia was the eldest.
Fela, the youngest.

During an air raid,
   as the rest of us sat at our table
the two wandered
   toward the *Ambulanz.*
Inside,
no more than
bandages and iodine.
Not enough to help
   if one were really hurt.

But neither Bronia nor Fela
was hurt.

Inside,
beside the bandages and iodine,
   were scissors.

They'd told me their plan.
Fela slipped inside.
Bronia stood outside.
Fela slipped the scissors
up her sleeve.
Bronia stood watch.

What's going on here?
  the *Kapo* asked.
She has a headache,
  Bronia answered.
  I was looking for the doctor.
I was looking for aspirin,
  Fela said.

The *Kapo* scowled.
Get back to your work station.

Bronia and Fela
  did as they were told.
And slipped the scissors to me
  under the table.

Happy Birthday
Helene
Lena

Good and happy birthday
Eva Pany

Simple Things

Paper.
Scissors.
Pencil.
Glue.

Simple things we didn't have.
Simple things once taken for granted.

Stolen.
Bartered.
Traded.

Simple things brought great risks.

In the day of your birthday
Have a heart,
Look into a heart
Auschwitz 12/XII/1944
To my dear Fanni
Hanka

Freedom, Freedom, Freedom
Wishing on the day of your birthday
Mania M—
12/XII/1944

In Secret

I remembered
  a pad of paper and colored pencils,
  a string of paper dolls, precisely cut
from a long time ago.

I worked
in secret
away from prying eyes
  the *blockova*
  other prisoners
away from Fania.

No one could know.

For Fani L.
Laugh among the people, cry in hiding
Be light in dance, but never in life
In the day of your birthday, to remember
Mala
12/XII/1944
Auschwitz

May your life be long and sweet
Mazal

Assembly

I used my
   ration of bread
   mixed with water
   to make the glue.

I cut my
   pretty purple blouse
   to make a cover.

I used
   a red thread
   from a seam
   to embroider
   an *F* onto the cover.

I used
   a gray thread
   from a seam
   of my prison uniform
   to bind the Heart.

Freedom and luck
All the best wishes on the day
of your birthday
Hanka W.

In the occasion of your birthday
We wish you lots of luck and health
I wish you a fast freedom
Fela

Worth the Risk

I was not afraid.

It was all
worth the risk,
not to do as I was told.

All they could do
was kill me.

Faniecka
From the bottom of my heart
Health and freedom,
Berta

Virtue is [...] keep quiet and
that's our sacrifice
This is unfortunately
everybody's fate
Signed Cesia
12/XII/1944

Messages

The girls
passed the booklet
back and forth
in secret.

In the lavatory,
where gossip flowed
like water down the drain.

At the work station,
holding it on their laps
   so Fania could not see
   so the overseer
      and *Kapo* did not see.
Fearing
   dreading
the call of *Kontrolle!*
or *Sabotage!*

They signed
in native tongues.
   Polish
   German
   French
   Hebrew.

They signed
in secret.

I wish that all your wishes should
be fulfilled
(As well as our predecessors)
Irena

Fani
Learn all about human beings,
because they are changing
People who are calling you a friend today
will be talking
against you tomorrow
Blue eyes, red mouth
Dear Fani, stay healthy
Auschwitz
On the 12.12.1944
I wish you the best dear fani,
Ruth

Birthday Cake

Each girl
handed over
  a portion of her bread.

I molded
  kneaded
  shaped
  sculpted it
into a
round
cake.

Decorated it
with a small amount
of margarine
and marmalade.

When you get old, put your glasses on
your nose, take this album in your hand
and read my signature again,
My loved Fani,
Mina

Chapter 12

Fania

Happy Birthday!
I could not believe
That anyone
Had remembered
My birthday.
That anyone
Could have given me
A cake.
That anyone
Could have made
Such a gift.

For me!

A birthday filled with
Love,
What was now my family,
A present
And cake!

I was wrong,

Birthdays did belong
In Auschwitz
Where each new day
Should have been celebrated
As life renewed.

My heart unfolded.

The Heart

A treasure.

Cut into four hearts
  Like four-leaf clovers.
Folded
  Into one heart.
Opening
  Like origami.
Covered
  With pretty purple cloth.
Embroidered
  With my initial.
Small enough
  To fit in the palm of my hand.
Big enough
  To restore my faith.
Friends replacing
  The family I'd lost.

A reason to take risks.
A reason to keep living.

Keeping the Secret

I tucked the Heart
Under my arm,
   Under the coarse fabric
   Of my prison uniform
Next to my heart.

All day I passed
   Kapos,
   Overseers,
   Meisters
All night I passed
   SS guards,
   Blockova,
   Black Triangle girls
Like nothing had changed.

But everything had changed.

Mama, Papa, and Mushke
Were gone.
I didn't know about Leybl.
I was no longer a good girl.

My secret,
   Pressed against my heart,
Made
Me
Brave.

January

Winter
Was the worst season.

Spring brought the rains
    And what natural life
    Existed
    Burst forth,
    Mocked us
    With signs
    Of life.

Summer brought the heat
    And insects
    That sucked
    Moisture from
    Our souls,
    Infecting us
    With loss
    And disease.

Autumn brought winds
    And decay,
    The knowledge
    That everything
    Dies.

But the cold of winter
  Was the closest
  I came
  To the cold of
  Death
  While still
  Breathing.

Punishment

Estusia Wajcblum
Regina Safirztajn
Were dragged to the scaffold
  During morning *Appell.*

Do not show
The Germans
Your tears,
  Zlatka said.

I bit my lip
Until I tasted blood,
But watched dry-eyed
And then marched
Off to work.

Ala Gertner
Roza Robota
Were dragged to the scaffold
  During evening *Appell.*

Honor their memory
By being strong,
  Zlatka said.

I bit my lip
Until I tasted blood,

But watched dry-eyed
And then went to bed
And stared all night
At the cobwebs on the ceiling.

Evacuation

The winter wind
Blew in rumors.
The Red Army
Was closing in.

Kommandos
Left after morning
Appell.
More left
During the day.
Rows and rows
Marching
Out the gates
Surrounded by
   Guards,
   Guns,
   And dogs.

Where are they going?
   Guta asked.
I don't know,
   Zlatka answered.
Will we go too?
   Giza asked.
I don't know,
   Zlatka answered.

Life trickled out
Of the camp.
Only the *Muselmanns*,
    Too weak to move,
Remained.

What will happen
    To those left behind?
Bronia asked.
No one answered,
    We all knew.

We,
    The *Union Kommando*—
    Eleven hundred women—
Were among the last
To march
Out of Auschwitz.
After the day shift
Dismantled
All the machinery.

The March

The soldiers led us through
The gates of Auschwitz
For the last time.

In the dead of winter
With only
Our wooden clogs,
  Prison uniforms,
  Bowls,
  And
  Spoons.

But I carried the Heart.

In the Middle

Front of the line,
   Girls were beaten
   For amusement.

Back of the line,
   Dogs were set upon
   Girls who fell behind.

Zlatka,
Bronia,
Guta,
Giza,
And I
Stayed unnoticed.

Russian Roulette

Soldiers laughed,
    Made bets.

One bullet,
    Chamber spun.

Eyes roved,
    Spied a girl.

Gun pointed,
    Trigger pulled.

Soldiers laughed,
    Paid bets.

At Night

The soldiers watched us
As they ate their provisions.

Leaving us to
Forage for food
   Winter berries,
   Pinecones,
   Tree roots.
Shooting at us
If we went too far.

The soldiers took turns
Standing guard and
Sleeping wrapped in woolen blankets.

We dug through the snow,
Huddled together,
   Like a pack of animals,
On the icy
Ground.

I closed my eyes
Not knowing if
I would wake
In the morning.

All That Mattered

A girl in front of me
Stumbled to the ground.

Before the soldiers saw
A woman raised her up,
Slapped her face.

The girl gasped,
   Stood,
      Continued marching.

Why did you slap her?
   I asked.
Isn't it bad enough
That the Germans beat us?

She stopped,
   The woman said,
    A patient teacher
    Explaining a simple lesson
    To a stupid student,
So I slapped her.
Now she walks.

Living is the only thing that matters.

Five Steps at a Time

Too cold
  To hold my bowl and spoon,
  To feel my toes.

Too tired
  To breathe,
  To suck air in and blow it out.

Just five more steps,
  I told myself.
You can do it.
Just five more steps.

Leybl will be waiting.
He knows what happened
To Mama, Papa, and Mushke.
You must survive for him.

Now five more.
Then you can rest.
Just five more steps.

But there was
No rest.
Just marching
On.

Five steps at a time.
The Heart still beating under my arm.

As I Was Told

I ran
   When I was told to run.

I walked
   When I was told to walk.

I slept
   When I was told to sleep.

And wondered every day
   Why I was still alive.

Chapter 13

Zlatka

Vanishing Points

Wodzisław Śląski
  a small town on the German border
thirty-five miles
from Auschwitz.

Our numbers thinned.
I'd lost count
  of the souls abandoned
  by the side of the road.

I looked
into the horizon
train tracks running away
  growing smaller
  unending
and wondered
if it would ever end.

Another Train

Given no choice
we all boarded,
like the sheep the
soldiers assumed
we had become.
The train rumbled
onward. We all
rode in open
boxcars. No food,
water, shelter,
or warmth. Just a
bucket and the
winter's cold wind.

Miraculous Food

White.
Flaky.
Wet.
Cold.
Delicious.

Not manna from heaven.

Snow.

Ravensbrück

Four days
in the cattle cars,
   a new camp
   a new *Judenrampe*
   a new Selection.

Too hard for us
to stay together,
   on the death march
   on the train.

I didn't know
what happened to
   the French girls,
   most of the others.
Were they even alive?

How could we
have survived so much
only to have it end now?

Paraded before
guards and doctors,
   to the left

                                 to the right.

Malchow

I never knew
how long we stayed in Ravensbrück.
Time melted
then froze
  cold and unrelenting.
It could have been weeks
or months.

It was still cold
when we started
another march.
Forty-five miles
  in the north-German wind.
Thinking only
of putting
one foot in front
of the other
  five steps at a time.
No other choice.

Another armament factory
Malchow.
Buried underground
hidden from the planes
that flew overhead.

Who Would Arrive First?

In Malchow
at least there were *Blocks*
  crowded and filthy
but out of the freezing rain.

But there was
  no food
  or water.
We were all accustomed
  to starvation.
But no water
put us closer to
death
than we had ever been.

Having long lost
our bowls,
The girls and I
held spoons
out in the rain.
Too anxious to wait
until the spoon filled
we lapped up the drops
and smiled.

There was no work
in Malchow
either.
So still I wondered,
If they do not need us to work,
   do they need us at all?

The girls and I
waited for freedom
which would come from either
the Red Army
or
Death.

Another Day in April

The Red Army
drew close enough to hear.

The rumble of tanks
explosions of artillery
echoed through the spring air.
Drawing closer
every day.

My heart
nearly exploded
with joy
at the sounds.

Malchow was evacuated.
Another march
to nowhere.
No plan
No destination.

Soldiers
    as young as Iser,
more frightened
    than I,
ordered to march
us prisoners away.

Some women
  too weary to go on
left behind to a fate
worse than marching.

Every day I marched
was another day I lived.

Who's Frightened Now?

When planes flew overhead
the soldiers hid
    cowered under trees
muttering fears
of being captured
by the
Soviets.

When bombs fell
most of the soldiers ran away
    too frightened
            of capture
            of death.

The ones who stayed
paid little attention to us.

Fania
Bronia
Guta
Giza
and I
were too weak to think
    of escape
    or rebellion.
Only surviving.

We took turns
  standing guard
  over each other at night.

Death
watched us
  more closely than the soldiers.

A Heavy Price

I watched
a girl
cry,
hold her stomach,
and beg
a soldier
for something
to eat.

Later
the girl
had a
chocolate bar.

I didn't know
the price the girl
had paid for it.

The girl didn't share
simply swallowed it
in two bites.

That night
the girl
cried,
held her stomach,
and begged

the soldier
for help.

In the morning
she was dead.

On the Banks of the Elbe River

One night
bombs rained down
flashing bright
as day.

The soldiers fled.

For the first time
in longer than
any of us
could remember
   Fania
   Bronia
   Guta
   Giza
   and I
were not
watched
guarded
prisoners.

We were free.

But we did not have
   strength to walk another step
   or
   knowledge of where to go.

Guta found
a ditch.
Bronia and Giza found
planks of wood.
Fania and I covered
the ditch with the wood.
And we slept
  huddled together
in the ditch.

And Still

When the silence of sleep
settled
I heard a rustle of paper
   of whispers
   of promises.

Fania's silhouette
reached under her dress,
withdrew the Heart,
unfolded it,
   cradled it
as if it were
her beating heart.

She hugged it
   kissed it
   tucked it back
   under her arm.

The silence of sleep descended
but not before
I marveled
how Fania
had held on to the Heart for so long.

Freedom!

In the morning
 footsteps
 voices
 a language only
   Fania and I
 understood.

A Soviet soldier
stood over our ditch.

Children,
get out of that hole.
You are free.

He reached down
gently
pulled us
out of the ditch.

The Red Army

pushed onward
leaving the girls and me with
   water
     and directions to a village.

Go that way,
   the soldier said.
Away from the fighting.
You'll be safe.

We walked
   hand in hand
trying to ignore
the stares
the pointing
the distrust
   in the villagers' eyes.

Bronia knocked on a door.
Please—

The door
slammed shut.

A woman on the street
stared
eyes wide,

You are Jews?
   she asked,
pointing
at our yellow stars
   faded
   torn
   dirty.
I thought all the Jews were gone.

Inside her home,
   she had little,
but offered
   warm broth,
   water to drink,
   and water to wash.

Her little girl
was drawing
on a pad of paper with colored pencils,
   a strand of paper dolls, precisely cut.

Fania watched too.
Placed her hand
over her hearts
and smiled.

Chapter 14

Fania

Fear Again

Swarms of Soviet soldiers,
   Men made feral from war,
Looking for revenge,
   Glory,
Anything to fill the holes
Where their hearts had once been,
Leered at us
With hunger.
I cringed,
   Wondering,
At a hollowness
That made scrawny
   Filthy
   Sick
Girls
Look good enough to eat.

Other survivors
   Men

Women
        Expressions vacant
        Gaunt
        Harrowed
Straggled into the village.
Ate whatever they could
    Grass
    Coal
    Chocolate
        From soldiers' rations
And died by morning
    In their own filth.

Chaos,
    As random as Auschwitz had been.
Villagers,
Soviet soldiers,
Survivors,
Without enough food
    Water
    Housing
    Sanitation.

Until the Red Army arrived.
Bringing doctors
    Nurses
    Tents
    Cots

Sheets
Medicine
Food ·
Life.

Field Hospital

In fields that once were pasture
Where cows grazed
Rows and rows of tents.
With clean cots
So soft
It was like floating.
And sheets
As white as the spring clouds.

I clutched the Heart
Unwilling, still,
To let it go.
Unwilling, still,
To admit that it existed.

Zlatka lay
In the cot beside me.
Bronia on
The other.
Giza and Guta
Nearby
Their muffled sobs
Came to me
Through the gauze of exhaustion.

Soldiers still leered
Until an officer appeared.

I didn't know his rank.
Didn't know his name.
He smiled.
I recognized him,
  Though I'd never seen him before.
He could have sat next to Leybl
  Studying *Torah*.
He could have stood to say the mourner's *Kaddish*
  For all he'd lost.

Are you a Jew?
  He asked.
I nodded.
Sholom aleichem
Peace upon you,
  He said.

Treatment

Doctors examined us
   Gently poked
   And prodded.
Nurses bathed us.
Kept us clean.
Let us sleep.
But we were not allowed
To eat.

Slowly
   A sip or two of broth.
   A tablespoon of mashed potato.
Though hunger gnawed
I knew,
I'd seen
What happened
When one rushed.

One sugar cube
Melted on my tongue.
A treat.
Sweetness
I'd forgotten
Existed.

It took weeks
To learn to eat
Again.

Visitors with clipboards
Moved through the rows
  Asking,
What is your name?
Where are you from?
Are you a Jew?

I answered their questions,
But they did not answer mine.
Where is my family?
Are they alive?
Where will I go?
What will I do?

It would take longer
To learn to live
Again.

Realization

It was the Russian officer
Who told me
What I already knew
   In my heart.

Do not expect to find them,
   He said.

It was the Russian officer
Who told me
What I could not make sense of
   In my head.

Not many survived,
   He said.

How?
   I wondered.
Did this happen?

Why?
   I asked.
Did I survive?
Why me?

He held my hand
Wiped my tears

And said,
Be thankful
You are alive.
You are free.

I crushed the Heart
To my heart.

Sometimes freedom is relative.

The Last Train

A transport
Poland.
stolen
Back to
had to
again.
Bronia,
Guta,
Friendship
in fear
Rumbled
tracks not
Allied
Wheels screamed
wreckage,
ruin.
million
Never
Never

back to
To lives
from us.
lives we
begin
Zlatka,
Giza,
And I.
forged
and love.
over
bombed by
forces.
at the
at the
Eleven
dead.
again.
again.

Never again.

Fania's heart, on display at the Montreal
Holocaust Memorial Centre

Glossary

Adonai—(Hebrew) Lord. Replaces the Hebrew letters *YHVH*, the Hebrew name of God, used in prayer.

Aktion—(German) Campaign. Term used to refer to an assembly and deportation of Jews to concentration camps.

Ambulanz—(German) First-aid station in the Weichsel Union Metallwerke.

Angel of Death—(Camp slang) Nickname given to Josef Mengele, SS captain, chief camp physician of Auschwitz II (Birkenau) from November 1943 to January 1945. Conducted inhumane medical experiments on prisoners in Auschwitz, most notoriously, though not exclusively, on twins.

Appell—(German) Roll call.

Aussenkommandos—(German) Work squads that did hard labor outside the camp.

Block—(German) A block of houses; barracks.

Block 11—Prison block where prisoners suspected of sabotage were held.

Block 25—Prison block used to house prisoners waiting to be taken to gas chambers.

blockova—(Polish/Slovak) Female prisoner in charge of a prison block.

Blocksperre—(German) Lockdown during large selections.

bubbe—(Yiddish) Grandmother.

chametz—(Hebrew) Leavened food forbidden during the Passover festival.

chuppah—(Hebrew) Canopy under which a bride and groom stand during their wedding ceremony.

Dayenu—(Hebrew) "It would have been enough." Refrain of a song sung at a Passover seder expressing thanks to God for gifts the Almighty has given.

the Days of Awe—Ten days between Rosh Hashanah and Yom Kippur, also known as the Days of Repentance. A time for self-reflection, examination, and repentance.

Judenfrei—(German) Free of Jews. Nazi term used to indicate that an area had been "cleaned" of Jews.

Judenrampe—(German) Jewish ramp. Located halfway between Birkenau and Auschwitz, the platform where transports disembarked from the trains and where prisoners underwent their first selection.

Judenrat—(German) Jewish council. Responsible for the internal government of the ghettos, enforced the laws imposed by the Nazis.

Kaddish—(Hebrew) Means "sanctification." Mourner's *Kaddish* is the prayer said for the dead by mourners; said only with a *minyan*.

Kanada—(Camp slang) Term used by prisoners to refer to the building where belongings confiscated from prisoners were sorted for shipment back to Germany. Became a black market where prisoners were able to buy small items—soap, pocketknives, sweaters, shirts, and material—with bread. Having items from *Kanada* was forbidden, punishable by confiscation, beatings, or worse. It was nicknamed *Kanada* because it represented a land of plenty far, far away.

Kapo—(German) Prisoner responsible for overseeing other prisoners.

Kiddush—(Hebrew) Prayer said over a glass of wine on *Shabbos* and on holidays.

Koje—(German) Bunk. Prisoners slept in three-tiered bunk beds.

Kommando—(German) Work squad.

Läuferin—(German) Runner, messenger.

Mach schnell—(German) Phrase that means "Hurry up."

mah nishtanoh—(Hebrew) Phrase that means "What is different?" Introduces the Four Questions, asked by the youngest person at a Passover seder.

minyan—(Hebrew) A quorum of ten Jewish adults (traditional observers required males, but progressive observers count females) for certain prayers.

mishpocheh—(Hebrew) Family, including relatives near and far.

Muselmann—(Camp slang) Living corpse.

"Next year in Jerusalem"—Phrase traditionally said at the end of the seder.

Passover—Jewish festival lasting eight days, beginning on the fifteenth day of the Hebrew month of Nisan. Commemorates the Exodus, when Moses led the Jews out of Egypt. During the festival certain foods that are leavened or may become leavened are prohibited. *Matzoh* (unleavened bread) is eaten instead of bread.

    seder—(Hebrew) Means "order." The festive meal held on the first two evenings of the Passover festival.

    seder plate—The plate that holds five symbolic foods:

        maror—(Hebrew) Bitter herbs (usually horseradish), which represent the bitter life of the Jews in slavery.

        karpas—(Hebrew) Greens (usually parsley) dipped in salt water to represent the tears of the Jews.

zeroa—(Hebrew) Roasted lamb shank bone. Represents the lamb sacrificed in biblical times to mark the doors of Jews so God would know to pass over those homes during the tenth plague (the killing of the firstborn).

beitzah—(Hebrew) Hard-boiled egg. Another symbol of sacrifice and a symbol of spring.

charoset—(Hebrew) Sweet mix of apples, cinnamon, and nuts that represents the mortar the Jews used to build Egypt.

afikomen—(Hebrew) A piece of *matzoh* broken at the beginning of the seder. Traditionally, the *afikomen* is hidden and the children search for it. A prize is given to the one who finds it. The seder cannot be concluded without the *afikomen*, so children can demand a high price.

Rosh Hashanah—Jewish New Year.

Sauna—(German) Bathhouse where prisoners were processed (registered, shaved, showered, deloused, and tattooed) once they arrived in Auschwitz.

Selection—Process used by SS doctors to decide who lived and who died.

Shabbos—(Yiddish) Day of rest. The holiday that begins every Friday night at sundown and ends at sundown on Saturday.

Sholom aleichem—(Hebrew/Yiddish) Phrase that means "Peace upon you." A traditional greeting.

Shema—(Hebrew) The most important of all Jewish prayers. A declaration of faith in one God.

shiva—(Hebrew) The week-long mourning period.

shmatte—(Yiddish) A piece of cloth used as a kerchief to cover the head.

shul—(Yiddish) Synagogue.

Sonderkommando—(German) Special unit. The squad of prisoners used to assist in the killing process and disposal of corpses.

SS—(German) Abbreviation for *Schutzstaffel*, "protection squadron." Paramilitary unit under Adolf Hitler and the Nazi Party. One of the most powerful organizations in the Third Reich.

Stube—(German) Room. Section of the block where prisoners lived.

tallis—(Hebrew) Ritual prayer shawl worn by men over the age of thirteen during prayers.

Talmud—(Hebrew) Word that means "instruction." A vast collection of rabbinic commentaries, debates, dialogues, and conclusions interpreting the Torah.

Tata—(Yiddish) Dad, Papa.

tateleh—(Yiddish) Diminutive used to address a little boy.

tefillin—(Hebrew) Small black leather boxes worn by observant Jewish men during morning prayers. The boxes are affixed with leather straps, one on the arm and one on the forehead.

Torah—(Hebrew) The Hebrew Bible. Consists of the five books of Moses: Genesis, Exodus, Leviticus, Numbers, and Deuteronomy.

Unetaneh Tokef—(Hebrew) Prayer recited at Rosh Hashanah and Yom Kippur.

Union Kommando—(German) Work squad for Weichsel Union Metallwerke.

verboten—(German) Forbidden.

Waschraum—(German) Washroom.

Weichsel Union Metallwerke—(German) Private factory in Auschwitz that made munitions for the Third Reich.

Yom Kippur—The Day of Atonement.

Zelt—(German) Tent. Infamous "living quarters" in Ravensbrück where hundreds of women were crammed without enough space to lie down.

What Is True?

The story of *Paper Hearts* is based on a true story. Twenty remarkable young women conspired against the Nazi regime—which classified them as subhuman, forced them to work as slave laborers, and thought of them as nothing more than the numbers tattooed on their arms—to commit an act of great defiance. They dared to behave as humans. They dared to behave as young women, to celebrate life—a birthday—with a simple gesture that, if they had been caught, could have meant death.

For my research I relied on the USC Shoah Foundation's audiovisual testimonies of Fania Fainer (Fania Landau) and Zulema Pitluk (Zlatka Sznaiderhauz), the film documentary *The Heart of Auschwitz* (Ad Hoc Films), the testimony given by Zlatka on the Montreal Holocaust Memorial Centre website, and several e-mail and telephone conversations with Fania's daughter, Sandy Fainer. Needless to say, some seventy years after the events, there are holes in the historical data. I remained as honest to the truth of the story as possible but filled the holes with stories I gathered from books written by other survivors, specifically of the *Union Kommando*, the *Sonderkommando*, the orchestra, and more general survivor stories from Auschwitz.

I did alter the time line to serve the story. Neither Zlatka nor Fania mention how they met. The Prużany ghetto, where Zlatka lived, was liquidated between January 28 and 31, 1943, and she describes her arrival at Auschwitz with her mother, younger brother, and sister in January 1943. The Białystok ghetto was liquidated on August 16, 1943, and Fania reports leaving Białystok the day prior to the liquidation. She then spent time in the Łomża Prison and Stutthof, and was transferred to Auschwitz at the end of 1943. I moved Fania's arrival at the camp up by several months to bring the girls together earlier in the story than they were in history.

Fania was the sole survivor in her family. Her mother, father, sister Mushke, and brother Leybl did not survive. Zlatka lost her mother, youngest brother, and sister in Auschwitz, as this story portrays. Her father and her brother Iser did not survive either. But Zlatka had three older siblings, two brothers and a sister, all of whom survived. I chose not to include them in this story, since they had left Poland prior to the war.

Auschwitz was a huge complex that comprised three large camps: Auschwitz I, Auschwitz II (Birkenau), and Auschwitz III (Monowitz). Auschwitz was the largest of the Nazi camps and rightfully earned the reputaton of being synonymous with terror and genocide. According to the United States Holocaust Memorial Museum in Washington, DC, and the Yad Vashem museum in Jerusalem, well over a million people were murdered in Auschwitz: at least 960,000 Jews; 70,000–

74,000 non-Jewish Poles; 23,000–25,000 Sinti and Roma; 15,000 Soviet POWs; and 25,000 additional civilians from other countries.

The *Weichsel Union Metallwerke* opened in October 1943. It was one of many privately owned industrial plants that contracted to use the prisoners of Auschwitz. Mala Zimetbaum and Edek Galinski escaped from Auschwitz in June 1944. They were captured in early July and publicly executed on September 15, 1944. Mala managed to cut her wrists as portrayed in the story. Several sources told a story of a woman who wrote a letter to her husband and was hanged, but did not identify her. I gave her the name of Mrs. Grosman. The *Sonderkommando* revolt of December 1944 and the role of the three young women who worked in the *Union Kommando* are as historically accurate as I could make them, given the constraints of a novel in verse. The death marches were real.

The messages inscribed in the Heart are real and appear as translated by the Montreal Holocaust Memorial Centre, with one exception—the last message. The translators were unable to read the handwriting on a few messages; those places are marked by ellipses. Two of the messages were unsigned. One was written while the girls were in Ravensbrück. It is not known where or when or who wrote the last message. The Montreal Holocaust Memorial Centre's translation of the message begins, "Near me are Zlatka, Fania, Bronia, Hela, and a lot of people which I know." The handwriting in the Heart is difficult to read, but for the sake of the story I changed the message, switching the name of *Hela* for *Fela*. A girl named Fela did sign the Heart, so it seemed like a reasonable assumption to make—though, as with so much about the Heart, there is much we do not know.

It is not known for certain how many of the girls who signed the Heart survived the death marches. After the war Zlatka, Fania, Giza, Guta, and Bronia returned to Poland together. They started their lives anew, met young men, fell in love, got married, moved away, and remained friends. Zlatka emigrated to Buenos Aires, Argentina, where she still lives today (as of October 2013). Giza, Guta, and Bronia emigrated to Israel and have since passed away. Carl Leblanc and Luc Cyr, creators of the documentary film *The Heart of Auschwitz*, were able to locate and interview Fela and Mina, both of whom were living in Israel at the time of the filming. Helene (one of the French girls) was found living in Cannes, France, but was unwilling to speak to the filmmakers.

Fania met her husband when she returned to Poland. They moved to Sweden for a time and then settled in Toronto, Canada, where they raised their daughter and son. Fania still lives there today.

Fania treasured her gift. She kept it secret during her imprisonment and carried it through the death marches for four months under unfathomable conditions. She kept the Heart with her when she was liberated, and through the years as she rebuilt her life and her family. In 1988 she donated the Heart to the Montreal Holocaust Memorial Centre, where it is on permanent exhibition, telling its story of defiance, love, and friendship to thousands of people every year.

Bibliography

Ash Luecker, Ltd. "Interactive Map of Auschwitz." BBC. Accessed July 29, 2014. http://www.bbc.co.uk/history/worldwars/genocide/launch_ani_auschwitz_map.shtml.

Auschwitz-Birkenau State Museum. "Auschwitz I." Accessed December 17, 2012. http://en.auschwitz.org.pl/h/index.php?option=com_content&task=view&id=6&Itemid=6.

Gross, David C. *English-Yiddish Yiddish-English Dictionary: Romanized.* New York: Hippocrene Books, 1995.

Fainer, Fania. *Visual History Archive.* Interview code 6010. USC Shoah Foundation.

Fainer, Sandy. Telephone interview by Meg Wiviott. March 18, 2011.

Fénelon, Fania, and Marcelle Routier. *Playing for Time.* New York: Atheneum, 1977.

Heilman, Anna. *Never Far Away: The Auschwitz Chronicles of Anna Heilman.* Calgary: University of Calgary Press, 2001.

Holocaust Education and Archive Research Team. "Sonderkommando Revolt—Auschwitz-Birkenau." Accessed December 17, 2012. www.holocaustresearchproject.org/revolt/sonderevolt.html.

Levi, Primo. *Survival in Auschwitz: The Nazi Assault on Humanity.* New York: Simon & Schuster, 1996.

Pitluk, Zulema. *Visual History Archive.* Interview code 16726. USC Shoah Foundation.

Saidel, Rochelle. *The Jewish Women of Ravensbrück Concentration Camp.* Madison: University of Wisconsin Press, 2004.

Shelley, Lore. *The Union Kommando in Auschwitz: The Auschwitz Munition Factory Through the Eyes of Its Former Slave Laborers.* Lanham, MD: University Press of America, 1996.

Steinbacher, Sybille. *Auschwitz: A History.* New York: HarperCollins, 2005.

The Heart of Auschwitz. DVD. Directed by Carl Leblanc. Montreal: Ad Hoc Films. 2010.

The Montreal Holocaust Memorial Centre website. Accessed April 7, 2013. http://www.mhmc.ca/en.

United States Holocaust Memorial Museum. *Holocaust Encyclopedia.* "Auschwitz." Accessed July 31, 2014. http://www.ushmm.org/wlc/en/article.php?ModuleId=10005189.

———. *Holocaust Encyclopedia.* "Death Marches." http://www.ushmm.org/wlc/en/article.php?ModuleId=10005162. Accessed March 7, 2013.

———. *Holocaust Encyclopedia.* "Josef Mengele." Accessed July 30, 2014. http://www.ushmm.org/wlc/en/article.php?ModuleId=10007060.

―――. *Holocaust Encyclopedia.* "Ravensbrück." Accessed March 7, 2011. http://www.ushmm.org/wlc/en/article. php?ModuleId=10005199.

―――. *Holocaust Encyclopedia.* "Ravensbrück—Oral History: Ruth Meyerowitz." Interview, 1990. Accessed May 15, 2013. http://www.ushmm.org/wlc/en/media_ oi.php?ModuleId=10005199&MediaId=2490.

Venezia, Shlomo, Béatrice Prasquier, and Jean Mouttapa. *Inside the Gas Chambers: Eight Months in the Sonderkommando of Auschwitz.* Cambridge, UK: Polity, 2009.

Yad Vashem. *The Holocaust.* "The Implementation of the Final Solution: Auschwitz-Birkenau Extermination Camp." Accessed July 31, 2014. http://www.yadvashem.org/yv/en/holocaust/about/05/ auschwitz_birkenau.asp